EX LIBRIS

University of Liverpool

Withdrawn from stock

VINTAGE **CLASSICS**

GEORGE SAUNDERS

George Saunders was born in 1958 in Texas and trained as a geophysical engineer. In 1988, he obtained an MA in creative writing from Syracuse University where he now teaches on the MFA program. His works comprise several collections of short stories, including *Tenth of December* (2013) which won both the inaugural Folio Prize and the 2013 PEN/Award for Excellence in the Short Story; a novella, *The Brief and Frightening Reign of Phil* (2005); a book of essays, *The Braindead Megaphone* and the *New York Times* bestselling children's book, *The Very Persistent Gappers of Frip*. He also writes regularly for the *New Yorker, Harper's, Esquire, GQ,* and the *New York Times Magazine*. In 2006 Saunders was awarded a MacArthur Foundation Fellowship and a Guggenheim Fellowship. In 2009 he received an Academy Award from the American Academy of Arts and Letters. George Saunders lives in Rochester, US, with his wife and children.

GEORGE SAUNDERS

CivilWarLand in Bad Decline

Stories and a Novella

VINTAGE

5 7 9 10 8 6 4

Vintage
20 Vauxhall Bridge Road,
London SW1V 2SA

Vintage Classics is part of the Penguin Random House
group of companies whose addresses can be found at
global.penguinrandomhouse.com

Penguin
Random House
UK

First published in Great Britain by Jonathan Cape in 1996

A CIP catalogue record for this book is available
from the British Library

ISBN 9781784871291

Typeset in India by Thomson Digital Pvt Ltd, Noida, Delhi

Printed and bound by Clays Ltd, St Ives plc

Penguin Random House is committed to a sustainable future
for our business, our readers and our planet. This book is made
from Forest Stewardship Council® certified paper.

MIX
Paper from
responsible sources
FSC® C018179

For
Mom, Dad, Nancy, and Jane
who taught me joy
and
Paula, Caitlin, and Alena
who completed it

Contents

CivilWarLand in Bad Decline

WHENEVER A POTENTIAL big investor comes for the tour the first thing I do is take him out to the transplanted Erie Canal Lock. We've got a good ninety feet of actual Canal out there and a well-researched dioramic of a coolie campsite. Were our faces ever red when we found out it was actually the Irish who built the Canal. We've got no budget to correct, so every fifteen minutes or so a device in the bunkhouse gives off the approximate aroma of an Oriental meal.

Today my possible Historical Reconstruction Associate is Mr. Haberstrom, founder of Burn'n'Learn. Burn'n'Learn is national. Their gimmick is a fully stocked library on the premises and as you tan you call out the name of any book you want to these high-school girls on roller skates. As we walk up the trail he's wearing a sweatsuit and smoking a cigar and I tell him I admire his acumen. I tell him some men are dreamers and others are doers. He asks which am I and I say let's face it, I'm basically the guy who leads the dreamers up the trail to view the Canal Segment. He likes that. He says I have a good head on my shoulders. He touches my arm and says he's hot to spend some reflective moments at the Canal because his great-grandfather was a barge guider way back when who got killed by a donkey. When we reach the clearing he gets all emotional and bolts off through the

1

gambling plaster Chinese. Not to be crass but I sense an impending sizable contribution.

When I come up behind him however I see that once again the gangs have been at it with their spray cans, all over my Lock. Haberstrom takes a nice long look. Then he pokes me with the spitty end of his cigar and says not with his money I don't, and storms back down the trail.

I stand there alone a few minutes. The last thing I need is some fat guy's spit on my tie. I think about quitting. Then I think about my last degrading batch of résumés. Two hundred send-outs and no nibbles. My feeling is that prospective employers are put off by the fact that I was a lowly Verisimilitude Inspector for nine years with no promotions. I think of my car payment. I think of how much Marcus and Howie love the little playhouse I'm still paying off. Once again I decide to eat my pride and sit tight.

So I wipe off my tie with a leaf and start down to break the Haberstrom news to Mr. Alsuga.

Mr. A's another self-made man. He cashed in on his love of history by conceptualizing CivilWarLand in his spare time. He started out with just a settler's shack and one Union costume and now has considerable influence in Rotary.

His office is in City Hall. He agrees that the gangs are getting out of hand. Last month they wounded three Visitors and killed a dray horse. Several of them encircled and made fun of Mrs. Dugan in her settler outfit as she was taking her fresh-baked bread over to the simulated Towne Meeting. No way they're paying admission, so they're either tunneling in or coming in over the retaining wall.

Mr. Alsuga believes the solution to the gang problem is Teen Groups. I tell him that's basically what a gang is, a Teen Group. But he says how can it be a Teen Group without an adult mentor with a special skill, like whittling? Mr. Alsuga

2

whittles. Once he gave an Old Tyme Skills Seminar on it in the Blacksmith Shoppe. It was poorly attended. All he got was two widowers and a chess-club type no gang would have wanted anyway. And myself. I attended. Evelyn called me a bootlicker, but I attended. She called me a bootlicker, and I told her she'd better bear in mind which side of the bread her butter was on. She said whichever side it was on it wasn't enough to shake a stick at. She's always denigrating my paystub. I came home from the Seminar with this kind of whittled duck. She threw it away the next day because she said she thought it was an acorn. It looked nothing like an acorn. As far as I'm concerned she threw it away out of spite. It made me livid and twice that night I had to step into a closet and perform my Hatred Abatement Breathing.

But that's neither here nor there.

Mr. Alsuga pulls out the summer stats. We're in the worst attendance decline in ten years. If it gets any worse, staff is going to be let go in droves. He gives me a meaningful look. I know full well I'm not one of his key players. Then he asks who we have that might be willing to fight fire with fire.

I say: I could research it.

He says: Why don't you research it?

So I go research it.

SYLVIA LOOMIS IS the queen of info. It's in her personality. She enjoys digging up dirt on people. She calls herself an S&M buff in training. She's still too meek to go whole hog, so when she parties at the Make Me Club on Airport Road she limits herself to walking around talking mean while wearing kiddie handcuffs. But she's good at what she does, which is Security. It was Sylvia who identified the part-timer systematically crapping in the planters in the Gift Acquisition Center and Sylvia who figured out it was Phil in Grounds leaving obscene messages for the Teen Belles on MessageMinder. She has access to all records. I ask can she identify current employees with a history of violence. She says she can if I buy her lunch.

We decide to eat in-Park. We go over to Nate's Saloon. Sylvia says don't spread it around but two of the nine cancan girls are knocked up. Then she pulls out her folder and says that according to her review of the data, we have a pretty tame bunch on our hands. The best she can do is Ned Quinn. His records indicate that while in high school he once burned down a storage shed. I almost die laughing. Quinn's an Adjunct Thespian and a world-class worrywart. I can't count the times I've come upon him in Costuming, dwelling on the gory details of his Dread Disease Rider. He's a failed actor who won't stop trying. He says this is the only job he could find that would allow him to continue to develop his craft. Because he's ugly as sin he specializes in roles that require masks, such as Humpty-Dumpty during Mother Goose Days.

I report back to Mr. Alsuga and he says Quinn may not be much but he's all we've got. Quinn's dirt-poor with six kids and Mr. A says that's a plus, as we'll need someone between a rock and a hard place. What he suggests we do is equip the Desperate Patrol with live ammo and put Quinn in charge. The Desperate Patrol limps along under floodlights as the night's crowning event. We've costumed them to resemble troops who've been in the field too long. We used actual Gettysburg photos. The climax of the Patrol is a re-enacted partial rebellion, quelled by a rousing speech. After the speech the boys take off their hats and put their arms around each other and sing "I Was Born Under a Wandering Star." Then there's fireworks and the Parade of Old-Fashioned Conveyance. Then we clear the place out and go home.

"Why not confab with Quinn?" Mr. A says. "Get his input and feelings."

4

"I was going to say that," I say.

I look up the Thespian Center's SpeedDial extension and a few minutes later Quinn's bounding up the steps in the Wounded Grizzly suit.

"Desperate Patrol?" Mr. A says as Quinn sits down. "Any interest on your part?"

"Love it," Quinn says. "Excellent." He's been trying to get on Desperate Patrol for years. It's considered the pinnacle by the Thespians because of the wealth of speaking parts. He's so excited he's shifting around in his seat and getting some of his paw blood on Mr. A's nice cane chair.

"The gangs in our park are a damn blight," Mr. A says. "I'm talking about meeting force with force. Something in it for you? Oh yes."

"I'd like to see Quinn give the rousing speech myself," I say.

"Societal order," Mr. A says. "Sustaining the lifeblood of this goddamned park we've all put so much of our hearts into."

"He's not just free-associating," I say.

"I'm not sure I get it," Quinn says.

"What I'm suggesting is live ammo in your weapon only," Mr. A says. "Fire at your discretion. You see an unsavory intruder, you shoot at his feet. Just give him a scare. Nobody gets hurt. An additional two bills a week is what I'm talking."

"I'm an actor," Quinn says.

"Quinn's got kids," I say. "He knows the value of a buck."

"This is acting of the highest stripe," Mr. A says. "Act like a mercenary."

"Go for it on a trial basis," I say.

"I'm not sure I get it," Quinn says. "But jeez, that's good money."

"Superfantastic," says Mr. A.

*

5

NEXT EVENING MR. A and I go over the Verisimilitude Irregularities List. We've been having some heated discussions about our bird-species percentages. Mr. Grayson, Staff Ornithologist, has recently recalculated and estimates that to accurately approximate the 1865 bird population we'll need to eliminate a couple hundred orioles or so. He suggests using air guns or poison. Mr. A says that, in his eyes, in fiscally troubled times, an ornithologist is a luxury, and this may be the perfect time to send Grayson packing. I like Grayson. He went way overboard on Howie's baseball candy. But I've got me and mine to think of. So I call Grayson in. Mr. A says did you botch the initial calculation or were you privy to new info. Mr. Grayson admits it was a botch. Mr. A sends him out into the hall and we confab.

"You'll do the telling," Mr. A says. "I'm getting too old for cruelty."

He takes his walking stick and beeper and says he'll be in the Great Forest if I need him.

I call Grayson back in and let him go, and hand him Kleenexes and fend off a few blows and almost before I know it he's reeling out the door and I go grab a pita.

Is this the life I envisioned for myself? My God no. I wanted to be a high jumper. But I have two of the sweetest children ever born. I go in at night and look at them in their fairly expensive sleepers and think: There are a couple of kids who don't need to worry about freezing to death or being cast out to the wolves. You should see their little eyes light up when I bring home a treat. They may not know the value of a dollar, but it's my intention to see that they never need to.

I'm filling out Grayson's Employee Retrospective when I hear gunshots from the perimeter. I run out and there's Quinn and a few of his men tied to the cannon. The gang guys took Quinn's pants and put some tiny notches in his

6

penis with their knives. I free Quinn and tell him to get over to the Infirmary to guard against infection. He's absolutely shaking and can hardly walk, so I wrap him up in a Confederate flag and call over a hay cart and load him in.

When I tell Mr. A he says: Garbage in, garbage out, and that we were idiots for expecting a milquetoast to save our rears.

We decide to leave the police out of it because of the possible bad PR. So we give Quinn the rest of the week off and promise to let him play Grant now and then, and that's that.

WHEN VISITORS FIRST come in there's this cornball part where they sit in this kind of spaceship and supposedly get blasted into space and travel faster than the speed of light and end up in 1865. The unit's dated. The helmets we distribute look like bowls and all the paint's peeling off. I've argued and argued that we need to update. But in the midst of a budget crunch one can't necessarily hang the moon. When the tape of space sounds is over and the walls stop shaking, we pass out the period costumes. We try not to offend anyone, liability law being what it is. We distribute the slave and Native American roles equitably among racial groups. Anyone is free to request a different identity at any time. In spite of our precautions, there's a Herlicher in every crowd. He's the guy who sued us last fall for making him hangman. He claimed that for weeks afterwards he had nightmares and because he wasn't getting enough sleep botched a big contract by sending an important government buyer a load of torn pool liners. Big deal, is my feeling. But he's suing us for fifty grand for emotional stress because the buyer ridiculed him in front of his co-workers. Whenever he comes in we make him sheriff but he won't back down an inch.

Mr. A calls me into his office and says he's got bad news and bad news, and which do I want first. I say the bad news. First off, he says, the gangs have spraypainted a picture of Quinn's notched penis on the side of the Everly Mansion. Second, last Friday's simulated frontier hunt has got us in hot water, because apparently some of the beef we toughen up to resemble buffalo meat was tainted, and the story's going in the Sunday supplement. And finally, the verdict's come in on the Herlicher case and we owe that goofball a hundred grand instead of fifty because the pinko judge empathized.

I wait for him to say I'm fired but instead he breaks down in tears. I pat his back and mix him a drink. He says why don't I join him. So I join him.

"It doesn't look good," he says, "for men like you and I."

"No it doesn't," I say.

"All I wanted to do," he says, "was to give the public a meaningful perspective on a historical niche I've always found personally fascinating."

"I know what you mean," I say.

At eleven the phone rings. It's Maurer in Refuse Control calling to say that the gangs have set fire to the Anglican Church. That structure cost upwards of ninety thousand to transport from Clydesville and refurbish. We can see the flames from Mr. A's window.

"Oh Christ!" Mr. A says. "If I could kill those kids I would kill those kids. One shouldn't desecrate the dream of another individual in the fashion in which they have mine."

"I know it," I say.

We drink and drink and finally he falls asleep on his office couch.

ON THE WAY to my car I keep an eye out for the ghostly McKinnon family. Back in the actual 1860s all this land was

8

theirs. Their homestead's long gone but our records indicate that it was located near present-day Information Hoedown. They probably never saw this many buildings in their entire lives. They don't realize we're chronically slumming, they just think the valley's prospering. Something bad must have happened to them because their spirits are always wandering around at night looking dismayed.

Tonight I find the Mrs. doing wash by the creek. She sees me coming and asks if she can buy my boots. Machine stitching amazes her. I ask how are the girls. She says Maribeth has been sad because no appropriate boy ever died in the valley so she's doomed to loneliness forever. Maribeth is a homely sincere girl who glides around mooning and pining and reading bad poetry chapbooks. Whenever we keep the Park open late for high-school parties, she's in her glory. There was one kid who was able to see her and even got a crush on her, but when he finally tried to kiss her near Hostelry and found out she was spectral it just about killed him. I slipped him a fifty and told him to keep it under wraps. As far as I know he's still in therapy. I realize I should have come forward but they probably would have nut-hutted me, and then where would my family be?

The Mrs. says what Maribeth needs is choir practice followed by a nice quilting bee. In better times I would have taken the quilting-bee idea and run with it. But now there's no budget. That's basically how I finally moved up from Verisimilitude Inspector to Special Assistant, by lifting ideas from the McKinnons. The Mrs. likes me because after she taught me a few obscure 1800s ballads and I parlayed them into Individual Achievement Awards, I bought her a Rubik's Cube. To her, colored plastic is like something from Venus. The Mr. has kind of warned me away from her a couple of times. He doesn't trust me. He thinks the Rubik's Cube is the devil's work. I've brought him lighters and *Playboy*s and once I even dragged out Howie's little synth and the mobile battery pak. I set the synth for carillon and played it from behind a bush. I could tell he was tickled, but he stonewalled. It's too bad I can't make an inroad because he was at Antietam and could be a gold mine of war info. He came back from the war and a year later died in his cornfield, which is now Parking. So he spends most of his time out there calling the cars Beelzebubs and kicking their tires.

Tonight he's walking silently up and down the rows. I get out to my KCar and think oh jeez, I've locked the keys in. The Mr. sits down at the base of the A3 lightpole and asks did I see the fire and do I realize it was divine retribution for my slovenly moral state. I say thank you very much. No way I'm telling him about the gangs. He can barely handle the concept of women wearing trousers. Finally I give up on prying the window down and go call Evelyn for the spare set. While I wait for her I sit on the hood and watch the stars. The Mr. watches them too. He says there are fewer than when he was a boy. He says that even the heavens have fallen into disrepair. I think about explaining smog to him but then Evelyn pulls up.

She's wearing her bathrobe and as soon as she gets out starts with the lip. Howie and Marcus are asleep in the back. The Mr. says it's part and parcel of my fallen state that I allow a woman to speak to me in such a tone. He suggests I throttle her and lock her in the woodshed. Meanwhile she's going on and on so much about my irresponsibility that the kids are waking up. I want to get out before the gangs come swooping down on us. The Parking Area's easy pickings. She calls me a thoughtless oaf and sticks me in the gut with the car keys.

Marcus wakes up all groggy and says: Hey, our daddy.

Evelyn says: Yes, unfortunately he is.

*

10

JUST AFTER LUNCH next day a guy shows up at Personnel looking so completely Civil War they immediately hire him and send him out to sit on the porch of the old Kriegal place with a butter churn. His name's Samuel and he doesn't say a word going through Costuming and at the end of the day leaves on a bike. I do the normal clandestine New Employee Observation from the O'Toole gazebo and I like what I see. He seems to have a passable knowledge of how to pretend to churn butter. At one point he makes the mistake of departing from the list of Then-Current Events to discuss the World Series with a Visitor, but my feeling is, we can work with that. All in all he presents a positive and convincing appearance, and I say so in my review.

Sylvia runs her routine check on him and calls me at home that night and says boy do we have a hot prospect on our hands if fucking with the gangs is still on our agenda. She talks like that. I've got her on speakerphone in the rec room and Marcus starts running around the room saying fuck. Evelyn stands there with her arms crossed, giving me a drop-dead look. I wave her off and she flips me the bird.

Sylvia's federal sources indicate that Samuel got kicked out of Vietnam for participating in a bloodbath. Sylvia claims this is oxymoronic. She sounds excited. She suggests I take a nice long look at his marksmanship scores. She says his special combat course listing goes on for pages.

I call Mr. A and he says it sounds like Sam's our man. I express reservations at arming an alleged war criminal and giving him free rein in a family-oriented facility. Mr. A says if we don't get our act together there won't be any family-oriented facility left in a month. Revenues have hit rock bottom and his investors are frothing at the mouth. There's talk of outright closure and liquidation of assets.

11

He says: Now get off your indefensible high horse and give me Sam's home phone.

So I get off my indefensible high horse and give him Sam's home phone.

THURSDAY AFTER WE'VE armed Samuel and sent him and the Patrol out, I stop by the Worship Center to check on the Foley baptism. Baptisms are an excellent revenue source. We charge three hundred dollars to rent the Center, which is the former lodge of the Siala utopian free-love community. We trucked it in from downstate, a redbrick building with a nice gold dome. In the old days if one of the Sialians was overeating to the exclusion of others or excessively masturbating, he or she would be publicly dressed down for hours on end in the lodge. Now we put up white draperies and pipe in Stephen Foster and provide at no charge a list of preachers of various denominations.

The Foleys are an overweight crew. The room's full of crying sincere large people wishing the best for a baby. It makes me remember our own sweet beaners in their little frocks. I sit down near the wood-burning heater in the Invalid area and see that Justin in Prep has forgotten to remove the mannequin elderly couple clutching rosaries. Hopefully the Foleys won't notice and withhold payment.

The priest dips the baby's head into the fake marble basin and the door flies open and in comes a racially mixed gang. They stroll up the aisle tousling hair and requisition a Foley niece, a cute redhead of about sixteen. Her dad stands up and gets a blackjack in the head. One of the gang guys pushes her down the aisle with his hands on her breasts. As she passes she looks right at me. The gang guy spits on my shoe and I make my face neutral so he won't get hacked off and drag me into it.

12

The door slams and the Foleys sit there stunned. Then the baby starts crying and everyone runs shouting outside in time to see the gang dragging the niece into the woods. I panic. I try to think of where the nearest pay phone is. I'm weighing the efficiency of running to Administration and making the call from my cubicle when six fast shots come from the woods. Several of the oldest Foleys assume the worst and drop weeping to their knees in the churchyard.

I don't know the first thing about counseling survivors, so I run for Mr. A.

He's drinking and watching his bigscreen. I tell him what happened and he jumps up and calls the police. Then he says let's go do whatever little we can for these poor people who entrusted us with their sacred family occasion only to have us drop the ball by failing to adequately protect them.

When we get back to the churchyard the Foleys are kicking and upbraiding six gang corpses. Samuel's having a glass of punch with the niece. The niece's dad is hanging all over Sam trying to confirm his daughter's virginity. Sam says it wasn't even close and goes on and on about the precision of his scope.

Then we hear sirens.

Sam says: I'm going into the woods.

Mr. A says: We never saw you, big guy.

The niece's dad says: Bless you, sir.

Sam says: Adios.

Mr. A stands on the hitching post and makes a little speech, the gist of which is, let's blame another gang for killing these dirtbags so Sam can get on with his important work.

The Foleys agree.

The police arrive and we all lie like rugs.

*

13

THE WORD SPREADS on Sam and the gangs leave us alone. For two months the Park is quiet and revenues start upscaling. Then some high-school kid pulls a butter knife on Fred Moore and steals a handful of penny candy from the General Store. As per specs, Fred alerts Mr. A of a Revenue-Impacting Event. Mr. A calls Security and we perform Exit Sealage. We look everywhere, but the kid's gone. Mr. A says what the hell, Unseal, it's just candy, profit loss is minimal. Sam hears the Unseal Tone on the PA and comes out of the woods all mad with his face painted and says that once the word gets out we've gone soft the gangs will be back in a heartbeat. I ask since when do gangs use butter knives. Sam says a properly trained individual can kill a wild boar with a butter knife. Mr. A gives me a look and says why don't we let Sam run this aspect of the operation since he possesses the necessary expertise. Then Mr. A offers to buy him lunch and Sam says no, he'll eat raw weeds and berries as usual.

I go back to my Verisimilitude Evaluation on the Cimarron Brothel. Everything looks super. As per my recommendations they've replaced the young attractive simulated whores with uglier women with a little less on the ball. We were able to move the ex-simulated whores over to the Sweete Shoppe, so everybody's happy, especially the new simulated whores, who were for the most part middle-aged women we lured away from fast-food places via superior wages.

When I've finished the Evaluation I go back to my office for lunch. I step inside and turn on the fake oil lamp and there's a damn human hand on my chair, holding a note. All around the hand there's penny candy. The note says: Sir, another pig disciplined who won't mess with us anymore and also I need more ammo. It's signed: Samuel the Rectifier.

I call Mr. A and he says Jesus. Then he tells me to bury the hand in the marsh behind Refreshments. I say shouldn't we call the police. He says we let it pass when it was six dead kids, why should we start getting moralistic now over one stinking hand?

I say: But sir, he killed a high-schooler for stealing candy.

He says: That so-called high-schooler threatened Fred Moore, a valued old friend of mine, with a knife.

A butter knife, I say.

He asks if I've seen the droves of unemployed huddled in front of Personnel every morning.

I ask if that's a threat and he says no, it's a reasonable future prognostication.

"What's done is done," he says. "We're in this together. If I take the fall on this, you'll eat the wienie as well. Let's just put this sordid ugliness behind us and get on with the business of providing an enjoyable living for those we love."

I hang up and sit looking at the hand. There's a class ring on it.

Finally I knock it into a garbage sack with my phone and go out to the marsh.

As I'm digging, Mr. McKinnon glides up. He gets down on his knees and starts sniffing the sack. He starts talking about bloody wagon wheels and a boy he once saw sitting in a creek slapping the water with his own severed arm. He tells how the dead looked with rain on their faces and of hearing lunatic singing from all corners of the field of battle and of king-sized rodents gorging themselves on the entrails of his friends.

It occurs to me that the Mr.'s a loon.

I dig down a couple feet and drop the hand in. Then I back-fill and get out of there fast. I look over my shoulder and he's rocking back and forth over the hole mumbling to himself.

As I pass a sewer cover the Mrs. rises out of it. Seeing the Mr. enthralled by blood she starts shrieking and howling to beat the band. When she finally calms down she comes to rest in a tree branch. Tears run down her see-through cheeks. She says there's been a horrid violent seed in him since he came home from the war. She says she can see they're going to have to go away. Then she blasts over my head elongate and glowing and full of grief and my hat gets sucked off.

All night I have bad dreams about severed hands. In one I'm eating chili and a hand comes out of my bowl and gives me the thumbs-down. I wake up with a tingling wrist. Evelyn says if I insist on sleeping uneasily would I mind doing it on the couch, since she has a family to care for during the day and this requires a certain amount of rest. I think about confessing to her but then I realize if I do she'll nail me.

The nights when she'd fall asleep with her cheek on my thigh are certainly long past.

I lie there awhile watching her make angry faces in her sleep. Then I go for a walk. As usual Mr. Ebershom's practicing figure-skating moves in his foyer. I sit down by our subdivision's fake creek and think. First of all, burying a hand isn't murder. It doesn't say anywhere thou shalt not bury some guy's hand. By the time I got involved the kid was dead. Where his hand ended up is inconsequential.

Then I think: What am I saying? I did a horrible thing. Even as I sit here I'm an accomplice and an obstructor of justice.

But then I see myself in the penitentiary and the boys waking up scared in the night without me, and right then and there with my feet in the creek I decide to stay clammed up forever and take my lumps in the afterlife.

HALLOWEEN'S SPECIAL IN the Park. Our brochure says: Lose Yourself in Eerie Autumnal Splendor. We spray cobwebs around the Structures and dress up Staff in ghoul costumes and hand out period-authentic treats. We hide holograph generators in the woods and project images of famous Americans as ghosts. It's always a confusing time for the McKinnons. Last year the Mr. got in a head-to-head with the image of Jefferson Davis. He stood there in the woods yelling at it for hours while the Mrs. and the girls begged him to come away. Finally I had to cut power to the unit.

I drive home at lunch and pick the boys up for trick-or-treating. Marcus is a rancher and Howie's an accountant. He's wearing thick fake lips and carrying a ledger. The Park's the only safe place to trick-or-treat anymore. Last year some wacko in a complex near our house laced his Snickers with a virus. I drove by the school and they were CPRing this little girl in a canary suit. So forget it.

I take them around to the various Structures and they pick up their share of saltwater taffy and hard tasteless frontier candy and wooden whistles and toy soldiers made of soap.

Then just as we start across the Timeless Green a mob of teens bursts out of the Feinstein Memorial Conifer Grove.

"Gangs!" I yell to the boys. "Get down!"

I hear a shot and look up and there's Samuel standing on a stump at tree line. Thank God, I think. He lets loose another round and one of the teens drops. Marcus is down beside me whimpering with his nose in my armpit. Howie's always been the slow one. He stands there with his mouth open, one hand in his plastic pumpkin. A second teen drops. Then Howie drops and his pumpkin goes flying.

I crawl over and beg him to be okay. He says there's no pain. I check him over and check him over and all that's wrong is his ledger's been shot. I'm so relieved I kiss him on the mouth and he yells at me to quit.

Samuel drops a third teen, then runs yipping into the woods.

17

The ambulance shows up and the paramedics load up the wounded teens. They're all still alive and one's saying a rosary. I take the boys to City Hall and confront Mr. A. I tell him I'm turning Sam in. He asks if I've gone daft and suggests I try putting food on the table from a jail cell while convicts stand in line waiting to have their way with my rear.

At this point I send the boys out to the foyer.

"He shot Howie,' I say. "I want him put away."

"He shot Howie's ledger,' Mr. A says. "He shot Howie's ledger in the process of saving Howie's life. But whatever. Let's not mince hairs. If Sam gets put away, we get put away. Does that sound to you like a desirable experience?"

"No," I say.

"What I'm primarily saying," he says, "is that this is a time for knowledge assimilation, not backstabbing. We learned a lesson, you and I. We personally grew. Gratitude for this growth is an appropriate response. Gratitude, and being careful never to make the same mistake twice."

He gets out a Bible and says let's swear on it that we'll never hire a crazed maniac to perform an important security function again. Then the phone rings. Sylvia's cross-referenced today's Admissions data and found that the teens weren't a gang at all but a bird-watching group who made the mistake of being male and adolescent and wandering too far off the trail.

"Ouch," Mr. A says. "This could be a serious negative."

In the foyer the kids are trying to get the loaches in the corporate tank to eat bits of Styrofoam. I phone Evelyn and tell her what happened and she calls me a butcher. She wants to know how on earth I could bring the boys to the Park knowing what I knew. She says she doesn't see how I'm going to live with myself in light of how much they trusted and loved me and how badly I let them down by leaving their fates to chance.

I say I'm sorry and she seems to be thinking. Then she tells me just get them home without putting them in further jeopardy, assuming that's within the scope of my mental powers.

AT HOME SHE puts them in the tub and sends me out for pizza. I opt for Melvin's Pasta Lair. Melvin's a religious zealot who during the Depression worked five jobs at once. Sometimes I tell him my troubles and he says I should stop whining and count my blessings. Tonight I tell him I feel I should take some responsibility for eliminating the Samuel problem but I'm hesitant because of the discrepancy in our relative experience in violence. He says you mean you're scared. I say not scared, just aware of the likelihood of the possibility of failure. He gives me a look. I say it must have been great to grow up when men were men. He says men have always been what they are now, namely incapable of coping with life without the intervention of God the Almighty. Then in the oven behind him my pizza starts smoking and he says case in point.

He makes me another and urges me to get in touch with my Lord personally. I tell him I will. I always tell him I will.

When I get home they're gone.

Evelyn's note says: I could never forgive you for putting our sons at risk. Goodbye forever, you passive flake. Don't try to find us. I've told the kids you sent us away in order to marry a floozy.

Like an idiot I run out to the street. Mrs. Schmidt is prodding her automatic sprinkler system with a rake, trying to detect leaks in advance. She asks how I am and I tell her not now. I sit on the lawn. The stars are very near. The phone rings. I run inside prepared to grovel, but it's only Mr. A. He says come down to the Park immediately because he's got big horrific news.

19

When I get there he's sitting in his office half-crocked. He tells me we're unemployed. The investors have gotten wind of the bird-watcher shootings and withdrawn all support. The Park is no more. I tell him about Evelyn and the kids. He says that's the least of his worries because he's got crushing debt. He asks if I have any savings he could have. I say no. He says that just for the record and my own personal development, he's always found me dull and has kept me around primarily for my yes-man capabilities and because sometimes I'm so cautious I'm a hoot.

Then he says: Look, get your ass out, I'm torching this shit-hole for insurance purposes.

I want to hit or at least insult him, but I need this week's pay to find my kids. So I jog off through the Park. In front of Information Hoedown I see the McKinnons cavorting. I get closer and see that they're not cavorting at all, they've inadvertently wandered too close to their actual death site and are being compelled to act out again and again the last minutes of their lives. The girls are lying side by side on the ground and the Mr. is whacking at them with an invisible scythe. The Mrs. is belly-up with one arm flailing in what must have been the parlor. The shrieking is mind-boggling. When he's killed everyone the Mr. walks out to his former field and mimes blowing out his brains. Then he gets up and starts over. It goes on and on, through five cycles. Finally he sits down in the dirt and starts weeping. The Mrs. and the girls backpedal away. He gets up and follows them, pitifully trying to explain.

Behind us the Visitor Center erupts in flames.

The McKinnons go off down the hill, passing through bushes and trees. He's shouting for forgiveness. He's shouting that he's just a man. He's shouting that hatred and war made him nuts. I start running down the hill agreeing with him.

The Mrs. gives me a look and puts her hands over Maribeth's ears. We're all running. The Mrs. starts screaming about the feel of the scythe as it opened her up. The girls bemoan their unborn kids. We make quite a group. Since I'm still alive I keep clipping trees with my shoulders and falling down.

At the bottom of the hill they pass through the retaining wall and I run into it. I wake up on my back in the culvert. Blood's running out of my ears and a transparent boy's kneeling over me. I can tell he's no McKinnon because he's wearing sweatpants.

"Get up now," he says in a gentle voice. "Fire's coming."

"No," I say. "I'm through. I'm done living."

"I don't think so," he says. "You've got amends to make."

"I screwed up," I say. "I did bad things."

"No joke," he says, and holds up his stump.

I roll over into the culvert muck and he grabs me by the collar and sits me up.

"I steal four jawbreakers and a Slim Jim and your friend kills and mutilates me?" he says.

"He wasn't my friend," I say.

"He wasn't your enemy," the kid says.

Then he cocks his head. Through his clear skull I see Sam coming out of the woods. The kid cowers behind me. Even dead he's scared of Sam. He's so scared he blasts straight up in the air shrieking and vanishes over the retaining wall.

Sam comes for me with a hunting knife.

"Don't take this too personal," he says, "but you've got to go. You know a few things I don't want broadcast."

I'm madly framing calming words in my head as he drives the knife in. I can't believe it. Never again to see my kids? Never again to sleep and wake to their liquid high voices and sweet breaths?

Sweet Evelyn, I think, I should have loved you better.

21

Possessing perfect knowledge I hover above him as he hacks me to bits. I see his rough childhood. I see his mother doing something horrid to him with a broomstick. I see the hate in his heart and the people he has yet to kill before pneumonia gets him at eighty-three. I see the dead kid's mom unable to sleep, pounding her fists against her face in grief at the moment I was burying her son's hand. I see the pain I've caused. I see the man I could have been, and the man I was, and then everything is bright and new and keen with love and I sweep through Sam's body, trying to change him, trying so hard, and feeling only hate and hate, solid as stone.

Isabelle

THE FIRST GREAT act of love I ever witnessed was Split Lip bathing his handicapped daughter. We were young, ignorant of mercy, and called her Boneless or Balled-Up Gumby for the way her limbs were twisted and useless. She looked like a newborn colt, appendages folded in as she lay on the velour couch protected by guardrails. Leo and I stood outside the window on cinder blocks, watching. She was scared of the tub, so to bathe her Split Lip covered the couch with a tarp and caught the runoff in a bucket. Mrs. Split Lip was long gone, unable to bear the work Boneless required. She found another man and together they made a little blond beauty they dressed in red velvet and paraded up and down the aisle at St. Caspian's while Split Lip held Boneless against him in the last pew, shushing her whenever the music overcame her and she started making horrible moaning noises trying to sing along.

Maintaining Boneless cost plenty. Split Lip's main job was cop but on the side he sold water purifiers. When the neighborhood changed, the purifier business went belly-up. Split Lip said the niggers didn't care what kind of poison they put in their bodies. Truth was, the purifiers were a scam. Inside was a sponge and an electric motor connected to nothing. But without the purifier money he couldn't afford the masseuse who eased Boneless's bad pain and couldn't afford to have Mrs. Cavendish in. So before leaving for work he'd put Boneless on the floor with a water bottle and her lunch and a picture book. Halfway through his shift he'd call home and she'd jerk the phone to the floor by the cord and make a certain sound that meant she was fine. In her simple way she understood poverty and never asked him to leave work, and time and again he came home to find her shivering on the floor in soiled pants.

By this time the panic-sell was in full bloom. Old Poles and Czechs were losing their asses and leaving treasured flower gardens behind in a frenzy. Local industries failed left and right. The stockyard downscaled and Dad was reduced to pushing a gutcart for minimum. Even the nuns went racist after the convent was reappraised and it seemed their pension fund was in jeopardy. Dad resolved to sell. But it was too late. The moment was past. A big loss was in the cards. The realtor came over and said ten thou. Dad sat looking at him.

"I pour my life's blood into this place," he said, "and you offer me half what I paid?"

"Market forces at work," the realtor said. "But all right, all right. Call me a saint walking the face of the earth: ten thousand five."

"Get out," Dad said.

"Fine," the realtor said. "Live among the savages forever if you want."

"What's happening to me is a goddamned shame," Dad said, and threw a scratch pad at him.

"Agreed," the realtor said. "But don't blame me. Blame the spades."

Then it was spring, and flowers bloomed in the park.

Then it was summer and the lagoon scummed over and race riots broke out and tear gas blew over the trees as Leo and I fished for carp.

One day in June, Split Lip came into the clearing leading a black teen by the ear. We squatted in the reeds. Officer Doyle nudged the teen's little brother with his billy club. We knew the little brother. He was Norris Crane. He played cornet with me in school, in Amazing Marching Falcons. He was an altar boy whose skin tore like paper. The nuns said that because of his affliction he didn't have to kneel through Stations but he did anyway and offered it up to the Lord whenever he bled through his pants.

Officer Doyle said let's interrogate. Split Lip said I'll show you interrogation. He pushed the teen into the lagoon and held him under. With his club Doyle made Norris watch. The teen's hands slapped and slapped. Then Split Lip stood up and the dead teen floated.

Now that's interrogation, Doyle said.

Split Lip said to Norris: Tell a soul and I'll take it out on your fat-butt mom in a heartbeat.

We ran home crying. Dad said shut our mouths about it forever. Ma said pray continually and try to forget. But who could forget? Every day on the way to school we saw Norris outside Spritzer's, becoming the world's youngest wino. Old lady Spritzer sold to anybody. She was a bitter crone with a thick mustache and big arm veins who'd lost two sons to the Koreans and one to an aging Rush Street queen who brought him back by the neighborhood on weekends in a tremendous purple Lincoln. We'd see Norris puking into the sewer while talking nonsense about the blood of the Lamb and vowing in his high-pitched voice to waste Split Lip. Who would have believed him? He was twelve. He was a sweetheart who in

25

biology had hired Earl Dimps to carve up his fetal pig. Every Halloween he came to school an Apostle and proudly placed his papier-mâché staff in the aisle. Dead brother or no dead brother, his was a kind heart that would never allow him to do anyone harm.

Or so we thought. Then he came up with a gun. He showed it to us behind the Dumpster where Hal Flutie had lost his arm to the crushing blade.

"I can't live with it anymore," he said. "I'll sneak in there this morning and wait all day for him to come home."

"You won't," Leo said.

"I will," said Norris. "Nine o'clock tonight he dies."

At ten to nine Leo and I walked in the odd autumnal dark to Split Lip's sagging home. From the stockyard we could hear the Czechs inducing cows into the deathhouse with tongue clicks. When the tongue clicks didn't work they ran out extension cords and used the prods. We mounted the cinder blocks. Inside, Split Lip was doing I'm a Little Teapot, making a handle of his left arm and a spout of his right. Boneless applauded by pounding her wrists together. Overcome with love, Split Lip gathered her up in his arms.

"My darling girl," he said. "We'll stay together forever and every day will be fun like this. Would you like that?"

"Yunh," Boneless said.

"Would you like that my honeylamb?" Split Lip said.

"Yunh," Boneless said.

Norris stepped out of the closet, a frail kid in sneakers. He raised his gun and Boneless began to wail.

"Please no," Split Lip said. "Who will care for my child?"

Norris paused, thinking, then blew his own brains out across the yellow wall.

We ran. We ran to the train tracks and lay on our backs, sick in our guts as the guiltless stars wheeled by. After no dance would we look up at them happily now. Norris's soul whizzed through the highgrass. Chills broke out on my arms.

The Cranes moved back to Mississippi without a trace, reduced to a family of daughters.

Dad went almost blind, and evenings I'd guide him home from the stockyards telling him what color the sky was. Then one night Ma came home from Trim's Market with a broken arm and no groceries. Dad said take one goddamned guess at the race of the guys who did this. Leo and I sat there in the kitchen with big eyes as Ma made fruit salad one-handed.

Sick with rage, Leo joined the Nazis. Dad wept and said nobody liked the jigs, but that was no reason to go off the deep end. The next summer Leo cracked one in the head with a ball bat and Dad said enlist quick before they throw your ass in the clink. Leo lied about his age and soon sent from Parris Island a postcard of a hick woman with missile breasts. *I'm so fucking lonely for you, man,* he wrote. *Join up yourself and we'll go over and kick some ass together.*

But Dad had pledged me to Split Lip. They were old school pals. Since the shooting, Boneless had been a mess. Unless someone was there all the time she wept nonstop. Dad said that someone was to be me. By now he was a crazy blind guy stinking up the parlor. How was I supposed to tell him no?

So every morning I biked over and made her eggs and Split Lip went off to work, biting his lip in gratitude and offering me unlimited rides in his squad car. I came to care about her. She tried so hard. I read to her and taught her to type using a stick held between her teeth. I brushed her hair until it shone and made sure her smocks were clean.

Leo came home with a Baggie full of human ears and asked why was I wasting my life baby-sitting a tard. I said don't call her a tard. He said as long as I was being so pure, why

27

not give her the real scoop on her old man? I said because it would crush her. Boo hoo, he said.

Finally Split Lip died in his sleep. Father Delacroix read aloud the eulogy Boneless wrote. People wept at the level of her devotion and her beautiful choice of words.

Leo sat next to me half-crocked, whispering: Murderer, murderer.

With Split Lip dead the maw of the state home gaped. There invalids were frostbitten in their beds and lunatic women became pregnant without known lovers. Dad begged Ma to take Boneless in. But Ma said: Look at you, look at me, look at our son who's got no life, let her go where she can get proper care.

So in she went. Holidays we visited. At Thanksgiving Leo came along wired on speed and while I was out fetching turkey slices from the Olds told her all. I came back in and Ma was wringing her hands like a nut in the corner and Dad had Leo by the throat, asking where in the hell he'd left his sense of decency.

Leo pushed him off and said: Lies serve nothing. The truth serves God.

Dad said: God my foot, you buttinsky, you've broken her heart.

She looked up at me so sweetly I couldn't lie.

Thus was God served: a sobbing girl in a wheelchair, photographs of a dead man gathered up and burned, a typing stick used less often as the months went by, finally the cessation of all typing and a request that I visit no more.

Months passed. Nights I sat home, hearing gunshots and cackling addicts in the alley, waiting for any hopeful thing to sprout in my heart. Finally I thought: What can she do, throw me out? So I went over. When she saw me her eyes lit up. She typed and I talked until the sun rose and the halls filled with oldsters and lunatics hacking and grousing their way into consciousness. Then an ex-con with a head scar brought her a dish of eggs that looked like it had spent the night on a windowsill and I thought: Jesus Christ, enough is enough.

By then I was selling the hell out of Buicks at night. So I got a little place of my own and moved her in with me. Now we're pals. Family. It's not perfect. Sometimes it's damn hard. But I look after her and she squeals with delight when I come home, and the sum total of sadness in the world is less than it would have been.

Her real name is Isabelle.

A pretty, pretty name.

The Wavemaker Falters

HALFWAY UP THE mountain it's the Center for Wayward Nuns, full of sisters and other religious personnel who've become doubtful. Once a few of them came down to our facility in stern suits and swam cautiously. The singing from up there never exactly knocks your socks off. It's very conditional singing, probably because of all the doubt. A young nun named Sister Viv came unglued there last fall and we gave her a free season pass to come down and meditate near our simulated Spanish trout stream whenever she wanted. The head nun said Viv was from Idaho and sure enough the stream seemed to have a calming effect.

One day she's sitting cross-legged a few feet away from a Dumpster housed in a granite boulder made of a resilient synthetic material. Ned, Tony, and Gerald as usual are dressed as Basques. In Orientation they learned a limited amount of actual Basque so that they can lapse into it whenever Guests are within earshot. Sister Viv's a regular so they don't even bother. I look over to say something supportive and optimistic to her and then I think oh jeez, not another patron death on my hands. She's going downstream fast and her habit's ballooning up. The fake Basques are standing there in a row with their mouths open.

So I dive in and drag her out. It's not very deep and the bottom's rubber-matted. None of the Basques are bright enough to switch off the Leaping Trout Subroutine however, so twice I get scraped with little fiberglass fins. Finally I get her out on the pine needles and she comes to and spits in my face and says I couldn't possibly know the darkness of her heart. Try me, I say. She crawls away and starts bashing her skull against a tree trunk. The trees are synthetic too. But still.

I pin her arms behind her and drag her to the Main Office, where they chain her weeping to the safe. A week later she runs amok in the nun eating hall and stabs a cafeteria worker to death.

So the upshot of it all is more guilt for me, Mr. Guilt.

ONCE A NIGHT Simone puts on the mermaid tail and lip-synchs on a raft in the wave pool while I play spotlights over her and broadcast "Button Up Your Overcoat." Tonight as I'm working the lights I watch Leon, Subquadrant Manager, watch Simone. As he watches her his wet mouth keeps moving. Every time I accidentally light up the Chlorine Shed the Guests start yelling at me. Finally I stop watching Leon watch her and try to concentrate on not getting written up for crappy showmanship.

I can't stand Leon. On the wall of his office he's got a picture of himself Jell-O-wrestling a traveling celebrity Jell-O-wrestler. That's pure Leon. Plus he had her autograph it. First he tried to talk her into dipping her breasts in ink and doing an imprint but she said no way. My point is, even traveling celebrity Jell-O-wrestlers have more class than Leon.

He follows us into Costuming and chats up Simone while helping her pack away her tail. Do I tell him to get lost? No. Do I knock him into a planter to remind him just whose wife

31

Simone is? No. I go out and wait for her by Loco Logjam. I sit on a turnstile. The Italian lights in the trees are nice. The night crew's hard at work applying a wide range of commercial chemicals and cleaning hair balls from the filter. Some exiting Guests are brawling in the traffic jam on the access road. Through a federal program we offer discount coupons to the needy, so sometimes our clientele is borderline. Once some bikers trashed the row of boutiques, and once Leon interrupted a gang guy trying to put hydrochloric acid in the Main Feeder.

Finally Simone's ready and we walk over to Employee Underground Parking. Bald Murray logs us out while trying to look down Simone's blouse. On the side of the road a woman's sitting in a shopping cart, wearing a grubby chemise.

For old time's sake I put my hand in Simone's lap.

Promises, promises, she says.

At the roadcut by the self-storage she makes me stop so she can view all the interesting stratification. She's never liked geology before. Leon takes geology at the community college and is always pointing out what's glacial till and what's not, so I suspect there's a connection. We get into a little fight about him and she admires his self-confidence to my face. I ask her is that some kind of a put-down. She's only saying, she says, that in her book a little boldness goes a long way. She asks if I remember the time Leon chased off the frat boy who kept trying to detach her mermaid hairpiece. Where was I? Why didn't I step in? Is she my girl or what?

I remind her that I was busy at the controls.

It gets very awkward and quiet. Me at the controls is a sore subject. Nothing's gone right for us since the day I crushed the boy with the wavemaker. I haven't been able to forget his little white trunks floating out of the inlet port all bloody.

Who checks protective-screen mounting screws these days? Not me. Leon does when he wavemakes of course. It's in the protocol. That's how he got to be Subquadrant Manager, attention to detail. Leon's been rising steadily since we went through Orientation together, and all told he's saved three Guests and I've crushed the shit out of one.

The little boy I crushed was named Clive. By all accounts he was a sweet kid. Sometimes at night I sneak over there to do chores in secret and pray for forgiveness at his window. I've changed his dad's oil and painted all their window frames and taken the burrs off their Labrador. If anybody comes out while I'm working I hide in the shrubs. The sister who wears cateye glasses even in this day and age thinks its Clive's soul doing the mystery errands and lately she's been leaving him notes. Simone says I'm not doing them any big favor by driving their daughter nuts.

But I can't help it. I feel so bad.

We pull up to our unit and I see that once again the Peretti twins have drawn squashed boys all over our windows with soap. Their dad's a bruiser. No way I'm forcing a confrontation.

In the driveway Simone asks did I do my résumé at lunch.

No, I tell her, I had a serious pH difficulty.

Fine, she says, make waves the rest of your life.

THE DAY IT happened, an attractive all-girl glee club was lying around on the concrete in Kawabunga Kove in Day-Glo suits, looking for all the world like a bunch of blooms. The president and sergeant at arms were standing with brown ankles in the shallow, favorably comparing my Attraction to real surf. To increase my appeal I had the sea chanteys blaring. I was operating at the prescribed wave-frequency setting but in my lust for the glee club had the magnitude pegged.

Leon came by and told me to turn the music down. So I turned it up. Consequently I never heard Clive screaming or Leon shouting at me to kill the waves. My first clue was looking out the Control Hut porthole and seeing people bolting towards the ladders, choking and with bits of Clive all over them. Guests were weeping while wiping their torsos on the lawn. In the Handicapped Section the chaired guys had their eyes shut tight and their heads turned away as the gore sloshed towards them. The ambulatories were clambering over the ropes, screaming for their physical therapists.

Leon hates to say he told me so but does it all the time anyway. He constantly reminds me of how guilty I am by telling me not to feel guilty and asking about my counseling. My counselor is Mr. Poppet, a gracious and devout man who's always tightening his butt cheeks when he thinks no one's looking. Mr. Poppet makes me sit with my eyes closed and repeat, "A boy is dead because of me," for half an hour for fifty dollars. Then for another fifty dollars he makes me sit with my eyes closed again and repeat, "Still, I'm a person of considerable value," for half an hour. When the session's over I go out into the bright sun like a rodent that lives in the earth, blinking and rubbing my eyes, and Mr. Poppet stands in the doorway, clapping for me and intoning the time of day of our next appointment.

The sessions have done me good. Clive doesn't come into my room at night all hacked up anymore. He comes in pretty much whole. He comes in and sits on my bed and starts talking to me. Since his death he's been hanging around with dead kids from other epochs. One night he showed up swearing in Latin. Another time with a wild story about an ancient African culture that used radio waves to relay tribal myths. He didn't use those exact words of course. Even though he's dead, he's still basically a kid. When he tries to be scary he gets it all wrong. He can't moan for beans. He's scariest when he does real kid things, like picking his nose and wiping it on the side of his sneaker.

He tries to be polite but he's pretty mad about the future I denied him. Tonight's subject is what the Mexico City trip with the perky red-haired tramp would have been like. He dwells on the details of their dinner in the catacombs and describes how her freckles would have looked as daylight streamed in through the cigarette-burned magenta curtains. Wistfully he says he sure would like to have tasted the sauce she would have said was too hot to be believed as they crossed the dirt road lined with begging cripples.

"Forgive me," I say in tears.

"No," he says, also in tears.

Near dawn he sighs, tucks in the parts of his body that have been gradually leaking out over the course of the night, pats my neck with his cold little palm, and tells me to have a nice day. Then he fades, producing farts with a wet hand under his armpit.

Simone sleeps through the whole thing, making little puppy sounds and pushing her rear against my front to remind me even in her sleep of how long it's been. But you try it. You kill a nice little kid via neglect and then enjoy having sex. If you can do it you're demented.

Simone's an innocent victim. Sometimes I think I should give her her space and let her explore various avenues so her personal development won't get stymied. But I could never let her go. I've loved her too long. Once in high school I waited three hours in a locker in the girls' locker room to see her in her panties. Every part of me cramped up, but when she finally came in and showered I resolved to marry her. We once dedicated a whole night to pretending I was a household invader who tied her up. In my shorts I stood outside our sliding-glass door shouting, "Meter man!" At dawn or so I made us eggs but was so high on her I ruined our only pan by leaving it on the burner while I kept running back and forth to look at her nude.

What I'm saying is, we go way back.

I hope she'll wait this thing out. If only Clive would resume living and start dating some nice-smelling cheerleader who has no idea who Benny Goodman is. Then I'd regain my strength and win her back. But no. Instead I wake at night and Simone's either looking over at me with hatred or whisking her privates with her index finger while thinking of God-knows-who, although I doubt very much it's me.

AT NOON NEXT day a muscleman shows up with four beehives on a dolly. This is Leon's stroke of genius for the Kiper wedding. The Kipers are the natural type. They don't want to eat anything that ever lived or buy any product that even vaguely supports notorious third-world regimes. They asked that we run a check on the ultimate source of the tomatoes in our ketchup and the union status of the group that makes our floaties. They've opted to recite their vows in the Waterfall Grove. They've hired a blind trumpeter to canoe by and a couple of illegal aliens to retrieve the rice so no birds will choke.

At ten Leon arrives, proudly bearing a large shrimp-shaped serving vat full of bagels coated with fresh honey. Over the weekend he studied honey extraction techniques at the local library. He's always calling himself a Renaissance man but the way he says it it rhymes with "rent-a-dance fan." He puts down the vat and takes off the lid. Just then the bride's grandmother falls out of her chair and rolls down the bank. She stops faceup at the water's edge and her wig tips back. One of the rice-retrievers wanders up and addresses her as señora.

I look around. I'm the nearest Host. According to the manual I'm supposed to initiate CPR or face a stiff payroll deduction. The week I took the class the dummy was on the fritz. Of course.

I straddle her and timidly start chest-pumping. I can feel her bra clasp under the heel of my hand. Nothing happens. I keep waiting for her to throw up on me or come to life. Then Leon vaults over the shrimp-shaped vat. He shoos me away, checks her pulse, and begins the Heimlich Maneuver.

"When your victim is elderly," he says loudly and remonstratively, "it's natural to assume heart attack. Natural, but, in this case, possibly deadly."

After a few more minutes of Heimlich he takes a pen from his pocket and drives it into her throat. Almost immediately she sits up and readjusts her wig, with the pen still sticking out. Leon kisses her forehead and makes her lie back down, then gives the thumbs-up.

The crowd bursts into applause.

I sneak off and sit for about an hour on the floor of the Control Hut. I keep hoping it'll blow up or a nuclear war will start so I'll die. But I don't die. So I go over and pick up my wife.

LEON WANTS TO terminate me but Simone has a serious chat with him about our mortgage and he lets me stay on in Towel Distribution and Collection. Actually it's a relief. Nobody can get hurt. The worst that could happen is maybe a yeast infection. It's a relief until I go to his office one day with the Usage Statistics and hear moans from inside and hide behind a soda machine until Simone comes out looking flushed and happy. I want to jump out and confront her but I don't. Then Leon comes out and I want to jump out and confront him but I don't.

What I do is wait behind the soda machine until they leave, then climb out a window and hitchhike home. I get a ride from a guy who sells and services Zambonis. He tells me to confront her forcefully and watch her fall to pieces. If she doesn't fall to pieces I should beat her.

When I get home I confront her forcefully. She doesn't fall to pieces. Not only does she not deny it, she says it's going to continue no matter what. She says I've been absent too long. She says there's more to Leon than meets the eye.

I think of beating her, and my heart breaks, and I give up on everything.

Clive shows up at ten. As he keeps me awake telling me what his senior prom would have been like, Simone calls Leon's name in her sleep and mutters something about his desk calendar leaving a paper cut on her neck. Clive follows me into the kitchen, wanting to know what a nosegay is. Outside, all the corn in the cornfield is bent over and blowing. The moon comes up over Delectable Videos like a fat man withdrawing himself from a lake. I fall asleep at the counter. The phone rings at three. It's Clive's father, saying he's finally shaken himself from his stupor and is coming over to kill me.

I tell him I'll leave the door open.

Clive's been in the bathroom imagining himself some zits. Even though he's one of the undead I have a lot of affection for him. When he comes out I tell him he'll have to go, and that I'll see him tomorrow. He whines a bit but finally fades away.

His dad pulls up in a Land Cruiser and gets out with a big gun. He comes through the door in an alert posture and sees me sitting on the couch. I can tell he's been drinking. "I don't hate you," he says. "But I can't have you living on this earth while my son isn't."

"I understand," I say.

38

Looking sheepish, he steps over and puts the gun to my head. The sound of our home's internal ventilation system is suddenly wondrous. The mole on his cheek possesses grace. Children would have been nice.

I close my eyes and wait. Then I urinate myself. Then I wait some more. I wait and wait. Then I open my eyes. He's gone and the front door's wide open.

Jesus, I think, embarrassing, I wet myself and was ready to die.

Then I go for a brisk walk.

I hike into the hills and sit in a graveyard. The stars are blinking like cat's eyes and burned blood is pouring out of the slaughterhouse chimney. My crotch is cold with the pee and the breeze. The moon goes behind a cloud and six pale forms start down from the foothills. At first I think they're ghosts but they're only starving pronghorn come down to lick salt from the headstones. I sit there trying to write Simone off. No more guys ogling her in public and no more dippy theories on world hunger. Then I think of her and Leon watching the test pattern together nude and sweaty and I moan and double over with dread, and a doe bolts away in alarm.

A storm rolls in over the hills and a brochure describing a portrait offer gets plastered across my chest. Lightning strikes the slaughterhouse flagpole and the antelope scatter like minnows as the rain begins to fall, and finally, having lost what was to be lost, my torn and black heart rebels, saying enough already, enough, this is as low as I go.

The 400-Pound CEO

AT NOON ANOTHER load of raccoons comes in and Claude takes them out back of the office and executes them with a tire iron. Then he checks for vitals, wearing protective gloves. Then he drags the cage across 209 and initiates burial by dumping the raccoons into the pit that's our little corporate secret. After burial comes prayer, a personal touch that never fails to irritate Tim, our ruthless CEO. Before founding Humane Raccoon Alternatives, Tim purposely backed his car over a fat boy and got ten-to-twelve for manslaughter. In jail he earned his MBA by designing and marketing a line of light-up Halloween lapel brooches. Now he gives us the brooches as performance incentives and sporadically trashes a book-shelf or two to remind us of his awesome temper and of how ill-advised we would be to cross him in any way whatsoever.

Post-burial I write up the invoices and a paragraph or two on how overjoyed the raccoons were when we set them free. Sometimes I'll throw in something about spontaneous mating beneath the box elders. No one writes a better misleading letter than me. In the area of phone inquiries I'm also un-surpassed. When a client calls to ask how their release went, everyone in the office falls all over themselves transferring the call to me. I'm reassuring and joyful. I laugh until tears run down my face at the stories I make up regarding the wacky things their raccoon did upon gaining its freedom. Then, as per Tim, I ask if they'd mind sending back our promotional materials. The brochures don't come cheap. They show glossies of raccoons in the wild, contrasted with glossies of poisoned raccoons in their death throes. You lay that on a housewife with perennially knocked-over trash cans and she breathes a sigh of relief. Then she hires you. Then you get a 10 percent commission.

These days commissions are my main joy. I'm too large to attract female company. I weigh four hundred. I don't like it but it's beyond my control. I've tried running and rowing the stationary canoe and hatha-yoga and belly staples and even a muzzle back in the dark days when I had it bad for Freeda, our document placement and retrieval specialist. When I was merely portly it was easy to see myself as a kind of exuberant sportsman who overate out of lust for life. Now no one could possibly mistake me for a sportsman.

When I've finished invoicing I enjoy a pecan cluster. Two, actually. Claude comes in all dirty from the burial and sees me snacking and feels compelled to point out that even my sub-rolls have sub-rolls. He's right but still it isn't nice to say. Tim asks did Claude make that observation after having wild sex with me all night. That's a comment I'm not fond of. But Tim's the boss. His T-shirt says: I HOLD YOUR PURSE STRINGS IN MY HOT LITTLE HAND.

"Ha, ha, Tim," says Claude. "I'm no homo. But if I was one, I'd die before doing it with Mr. Lard."

"Ha, ha," says Tim. "Good one. Isn't that a good one, Jeffrey?"

"That's a good one," I say glumly.

What a bitter little office.

My colleagues leave hippo refrigerator magnets on my seat. They imply that I'm a despondent virgin, which I'm not. They might change their tune if they ever spoke with Ellen Burtomly regarding the beautiful night we spent at her brother Bob's cottage. I was by no means slim then but could at least buy pants off the rack and walk from the den to the kitchen without panting. I remember her nude at the window and the lovely seed helicopters blowing in as she turned and showed me her ample front on purpose. That was my most romantic moment. Now for that kind of thing it's the degradation of Larney's Consenting Adult Viewing Center. Before it started getting to me I'd bring bootloads of quarters and a special bottom cushion and watch hours and hours of Scandinavian women romping. It was shameful. Finally last Christmas I said enough is enough, I'd rather be sexless than evil. And since then I have been. Sexless and good, but very very tense. Since then I've tried to live above the fray. I've tried to minimize my physical aspects and be a selfless force for good. When mocked, which is nearly every day, I recall Christ covered with spittle. When filled with lust, I remember Gandhi purposely sleeping next to a sexy teen to test himself. After work I go home, watch a little TV, maybe say a rosary or two.

Thirty more years of this and I'm out of it without hurting anybody or embarrassing myself.

But still. I'm a human being. A little companionship would be nice. My colleagues know nothing of my personal life. They could care less that I once had a dog named Woodsprite who was crushed by a backhoe. They could care less that my dad died a wino in the vicinity of the Fort Worth stockyards. In his last days he sent me a note filled with wonder:

"Son," he wrote, "are you fat too? It came upon me suddenly and now I am big as a house. Beware, perhaps it's in our genes. I wander cowboy sidewalks of wood, wearing a too-small hat, filled with remorse for the many lives I failed to lead. Adieu. In my mind you are a waify-looking little fellow who never answered when I asked you a direct question. But I loved you as best I could."

What do my colleagues know of Dad? What do they know of me? What kind of friend gets a kick out of posting in the break room a drawing of you eating an entire computer? What kind of friend jokes that someday you'll be buried in a specially built container after succumbing to heart strain?

I'm sorry, but I feel that life should offer more than this.

As a child my favorite book was *Little Red-Faced Cop on the Beat*. Everyone loved the Little Red-Faced Cop. He knew what was what. He donned his uniform in a certain order every morning. He chased bad guys and his hat stayed on. Now I'm surrounded by kooks. I'm a kook myself. I stoop down and tell raccoons to take it like a man. I drone on and on to strangers about my weight. I ogle salesgirls. I double back to pick up filthy pennies. When no one's around I dig and dig at my earwax, then examine it. I'm huge, and terrified of becoming bitter.

Sometimes I sense deep anger welling up, and have to choke it back.

SADLY, I FIND my feelings for Freeda returning. I must have a death wish. Clearly I repulse her. Sometimes I catch her looking at my gut overhangs with a screwed-up face. I see her licking her lips while typing, and certain unholy thoughts go through my head. I hear her speaking tenderly on the phone to her little son, Len, and can't help picturing myself sitting on a specially reinforced porch swing while she fries up some chops and Len digs in the muck.

Today as we prepare mailers she says she's starting to want to be home with Len all the time. But there's the glaring problem of funds. She makes squat. I've seen her stub.

There's the further problem that she suspects Mrs. Rasputin, Len's baby-sitter, is a lush.

"I don't know what to do," Freeda says. "I come home after work and she's sitting there tipsy in her bra, fanning herself with a *Racing Form*."

"I know how you feel," I say. "Life can be hard."

"It has nothing to do with life," she says crossly. "It has to do with my drunken baby-sitter. Maybe you haven't been listening to me."

Before I know what I'm saying I suggest that perhaps we should go out for dinner and offer each other some measure of comfort. In response she spits her Tab out across her cubicle. She says now she's heard it all. She goes to fetch Tim and Claude so they can join her in guffawing at my nerve. She faxes a comical note about my arrogance to her girlfriend at the DMV. All afternoon she keeps looking at me with her head cocked.

Needless to say, it's a long day.

Then at five, after everyone else is gone, she comes shyly by and says she'd love to go out with me. She says I've always been there for her. She says she likes a man with a little meat on his bones. She says pick her up at eight and bring something for Len. I'm shocked. I'm overjoyed.

My knees are nearly shaking my little desk apart.

I buy Len a football helmet and a baseball glove and an aquarium and a set of encyclopedias. I basically clean out my pitiful savings. Who cares. It's worth it to get a chance to observe her beautiful face from across a table without Claude et al. hooting at me.

When I ring her bell someone screams come in. Inside I find Len behind the home entertainment center and Mrs. Rasputin drunkenly poring over her grade-school yearbook with a highlighter. She looks up and says: "Where's that kid?" I feel like saying: How should I know? Instead I say: "He's behind the home entertainment center."

"He loves it back there," she says. "He likes eating the lint balls. They won't hurt him. They're like roughage."

"Come out, Len," I say. "I have gifts."

He comes out. One tiny eyebrow cocks up at my physical appearance. Then he crawls into my lap holding his MegaDeathDealer by the cowl. What a sweet boy. The Dealer's got a severed human head in its hand. When you pull a string the Dealer cries, "You're dead and I've killed you, Prince of Slime," and sticks its Day-Glo tongue out. I give Len my antiviolence spiel. I tell him only love can dispel hate. I tell him we were meant to live in harmony and give one another emotional support. He looks at me blankly, then flings his DeathDealer at the cat.

Freeda comes down looking sweet and casts a baleful eye on Mrs. Rasputin and away we go. I take her to Ace's Volcano Island. Ace's is an old service station now done up Hawaiian. They've got a tape loop of surf sounds and some Barbies in grass skirts climbing a papier-mâché mountain. I'm known there. Every Friday night I treat myself by taking up a whole booth and ordering the Broccoli Rib Luau. Ace is a gentle aging beatnik with mild Tourette's. When the bad words start flying out of his mouth you never saw someone so regretful. One minute he'll be quoting the Bhagavad Gita and the next roughly telling one of his patrons to lick their own bottom. We've talked about it. He says he's tried pills. He's tried biting down on a pencil eraser. He's tried picturing himself in the floodplain of the Ganges with a celestial being stroking his hair. Nothing works. So he's printed up an explanatory flyer. Shirleen the hostess hands it out pre-seating. There's a cartoon of Ace with lots of surprise marks and typographic symbols coming out of his mouth.

"My affliction is out of my hands," it says. "But please know that whatever harsh words I may direct at you, I truly treasure your patronage."

He fusses over us by bringing extra ice water and sprinting into the back room whenever he feels an attack looming. I purposely starve myself. We talk about her life philosophy. We talk about her hairstyle and her treasured childhood memories and her paranormally gifted aunt. I fail to get a word in edgewise, and that's fine. I like listening. I like learning about her. I like putting myself in her shoes and seeing things her way.

I walk her home. Kids in doorways whistle at my width. I handle it with grace by shaking my rear. Freeda laughs. A kiss seems viable. It all feels too good to be true.

Then on her porch she shakes my hand and says great, she can now pay her phone bill, courtesy of Tim. She shows me their written agreement. It says: "In consideration of your consenting to be seen in public with Jeffrey, I, Tim, will pay you, Freeda, the sum of fifty dollars."

She goes inside. I take a week of vacation and play Oil Can Man nonstop. I achieve Level Nine. I master the Hydrocarbon Dervish and the Cave of Dangerous Lubrication. I cream Mr. Grit and consistently prohibit him from inflicting wear and tear on my Pistons. There's something sick about the amount of pleasure I take in pretending Freeda's Mr. Grit as I annihilate him with Bonus Cleansing Additives. At the end of night three I step outside for some air. Up in the sky are wild clouds that make me think of Tahiti and courageous sailors on big sinking wooden ships. Meanwhile here's me, a grown man with a joystick-burn on his thumb.

So I throw the game cartridge in the trash and go back to work. I take the ribbing. I take the abuse. Someone's snipped my head out of the office photo and mounted it on a bride's body. Tim says what the heck, the thought of the visual incongruity of our pairing was worth the fifty bucks.

"Do you hate me?" Freeda asks.

"No," I say. "I truly enjoyed our evening together."

"God, I didn't," she says. "Everyone kept staring at us. It made me feel bad about myself that they thought I was actually with you. Do you know what I mean?"

I can't think of anything to say, so I nod. Then I retreat moist-eyed to my cubicle for some invoicing fun. I'm not a bad guy. If only I could stop hoping. If only I could say to my heart: Give up. Be alone forever. There's always opera. There's angel-food cake and neighborhood children caroling, and the look of autumn leaves on a wet roof. But no. My heart's some kind of idiotic fishing bobber.

My invoices go very well. The sun sinks, the moon rises, round and pale as my stupid face.

I MINIMIZE MY office time by volunteering for the Carlisle entrapment. The Carlisles are rich. A poor guy has a raccoon problem, he sprinkles poison in his trash and calls it a day. Not the Carlisles. They dominate bread routes throughout the city. Carlisle supposedly strong-armed his way to the top of the bread heap, but in person he's nice enough. I let him observe me laying out the rotting fruit. I show him how the cage door coming down couldn't hurt a flea. Then he goes inside and I wait patiently in my car.

Just after midnight I trip the wire. I fetch the Carlisles and encourage them to squat down and relate to the captured raccoon. Then I recite our canned speech congratulating them for their advanced thinking. I describe the wilderness where the release will take place, the streams and fertile valleys, the romp in the raccoon's stride when it catches its first whiff of pristine air.

Mr. Carlisle says thanks for letting them sleep at night sans guilt. I tell him that's my job. Just then the raccoon's huge mate bolts out of the woods and tears into my calf. I struggle to my car and kick the mate repeatedly against my wheelwell until it dies with my leg in its mouth. The Carlisles stand aghast in the carport. I stand aghast in the driveway, sick at heart. I've trapped my share of raccoons and helped Claude with more burials than I care to remember, but I've never actually killed anything before.

I throw both coons in the trunk and drive myself to the emergency room, where I'm given the first of a series of extremely painful shots. I doze off on a bench post-treatment and dream of a den of pathetic baby raccoons in V-neck sweaters yelping for food.

When I wake up I call in. Tim asks if I'm crazy, kicking a raccoon to death in front of clients. Couldn't I have gently lifted it off, he asks, or offered it some rotting fruit? Am I proud of my ability to fuck up one-car funerals? Do I or do I not recall Damian Flaverty?

Who could forget Damian Flaverty? He'd been dipping into the till to finance his necktie boutique. Tim blackjacked him into a crumpled heap on the floor and said: Do you think I spent nine years in the slammer only to get out and be fleeced by your ilk? Then he broke Damian's arm with an additional whack. I almost dropped my mug.

I tell Tim I'm truly sorry I didn't handle the situation more effectively. He says the raccoon must've had a sad last couple of minutes once it realized it had given up its life for the privilege of gnawing on a shank of pure fat. That hurts. Why I continue to expect decent treatment from someone who's installed a torture chamber in the corporate basement is beyond me. Down there he's got a Hide-A-Bed and a whip collection and an executioner's mask with a built-in

Walkman. Sometimes when I'm invoicing late he'll bring in one of his willing victims. Usually they're both wasto. I get as much of me under my desk as I can. Talk about the fall of man. Talk about some father somewhere being crestfallen if he knew what his daughter was up to. Once I peeked out as they left and saw a blonde with a black eye going wherever Tim pointed and picking up his coat whenever he purposely dropped it.

"You could at least take me for coffee," she said.

"I'd like to spill some on your bare flesh," Tim said.

"Mmm," she said. "Sounds good."

How do people get like this, I thought. Can they change back? Can they learn again to love and be gentle? How can they look at themselves in the mirror or hang Christmas ornaments without overflowing with self-loathing?

Then I thought: I may be obese but at least I'm not cruel to the point of being satanic.

Next day Tim was inducted into Rotary and we all went to the luncheon. He spoke on turning one's life around. He spoke on the bitter lessons of incarceration. He sang the praises of America and joked with balding sweetheart ophthalmologists, and after lunch hung his Rotary plaque in the torture chamber stairwell and ordered me to Windex it daily or face extremely grim consequences.

TUESDAY A CAR pulls up as Claude and I approach the burial pit with the Carlisle raccoons. We drag the cage into a shrub and squat panting. Claude whispers that I smell. He whispers that if he weighed four hundred he'd take into account the people around him and go on a diet. The sky's the purple of holy card Crucifixion scenes, the rending of the firmament and all that. A pale girl in a sari gets out of the car and walks to the lip of the pit. She paces off the circumference and scribbles

49

in a notebook. She takes photos. She slides down on her rear and comes back up with some coon bones in a Baggie.

After she leaves we rush back to the office. Tim's livid and starts baby-oiling his trademark blackjack. He says no more coons in the pit until further notice. He says we're hereby in crisis mode and will keep the coons on blue ice in our cubicles and if need be wear nose clips. He says the next time she shows up he may have to teach her a lesson about jeopardizing our meal ticket. He says animal rights are all well and good but there's a substantive difference between a cute bunny or cat and a disgusting raccoon that thrives on carrion and trash and creates significant sanitation problems with its inquisitiveness.

"Oh, get off it," Claude says, affection for Tim shining from his dull eyes. "You'd eliminate your own mother if there was a buck in it for you."

"Undeniably," Tim says. "Especially if she knocked over a client trash can or turned rabid."

Then he hands me the corporate Visa and sends me to HardwareNiche for coolers. At HardwareNiche you can get a video of *Bloodiest Crimes of the Century Reenacted*. You can get a video of Great Bloopers made during the filming of *Bloodiest Crimes of the Century Reenacted*. You can get a bird feeder that plays "How Dry I Am" while electronically emitting a soothing sensation birds love. You can get a Chill'n'Pray, an overpriced cooler with a holographic image of a famous religious personality on the lid. I opt for Buddha. I can almost hear Tim sarcastically comparing our girths and asking since when has cost control been thrown to the wind. But the Chill'n'Prays are all they've got. I'm on Tim's shit list if I do and on Tim's shit list if I don't. He has an actual shit list. Freeda generated it and enhanced it with a graphic of an angry piece of feces stamping its feet.

I buy the coolers, hoping in spite of myself that he'll applaud my decisiveness. When I get back to the office everyone's gone for the night. The Muzak's off for a change and loud whacks and harsh words are floating up from the basement via the heat ducts. Before long Tim tromps up the stairs swearing. I hide pronto. He shouts thanks for nothing, and says he could have had more rough-and-tumble fun dangling a cat over a banister, and that there's nothing duller than a clerk with the sexual imagination of a grape.

"Document placement and retrieval specialist," Freeda says in a hurt tone.

"Whatever," Tim says, and speeds off in his Porsche.

I emerge overwhelmed from my cubicle. Over her shoulder and through the plate glass is a shocked autumnal moon. Freeda's cheek is badly bruised. Otherwise she's radiant with love. My mouth hangs open.

"What can I say?" she says. "I can't get enough of the man."

"Good night," I say, and forget about my car, and walk the nine miles home in a daze.

ALL DAY WEDNESDAY I prepare to tell Tim off. But I'm too scared. Plus he could rightly say she's a consenting adult. What business is it of mine? Why defend someone who has no desire to be defended? Instead I drop a few snots in his coffee cup and use my network access privileges to cancel his print jobs. He asks can I work late and in spite of myself I fawningly say sure. I hate him. I hate myself. Everybody else goes home. Big clouds roll in. I invoice like mad. Birds light on the Dumpster and feed on substances caked on the lid. What a degraded cosmos. What a case of something starting out nice and going bad.

Just after seven I hear him shout: "You, darling, will rot in hell, with the help of a swift push to the grave from me!" At first I think he's pillow-talking with Freeda by phone. Then I look out the window and see the animal rights girl at the lip of our pit with a camcorder.

Admirable dedication, I think, wonderful clarity of vision.

Tim runs out the door with his blackjack unsheathed.

What to do? Clearly he means her harm. I follow him, leaving behind my loafers to minimize noise. I keep to the shadows and scurry in my socks from tiny berm to tiny berm. I heave in an unattractive manner. My heart rate's in the ionosphere. To my credit I'm able to keep up with him. Meanwhile she's struggling up the slope with her hair in sweet disarray backlit by a moon the color of honey, camcorder on her head like some kind of Kenyan water jug.

"Harlot," Tim hisses, "attempted defiler of my dream," and whips his blackjack down. Am I quick? I am so quick. I lunge up and take it on the wrist. My arm bone goes to mush, and my head starts to spin, and I wrap Tim up in a hug the size of Tulsa.

"Run," I gasp to the girl, and see in the moonlight the affluent white soles of her fleeing boat-type shoes.

I hug hard. I tell him drop the jack and to my surprise he does. Do I then release him? To my shame, no. So much sick rage is stored up in me. I never knew. And out it comes in one mondo squeeze, and something breaks, and he goes limp, and I lay him gently down in the dirt.

I CPR like anything. I beg him to rise up and thrash me. I do a crazy little dance of grief. But it's no good.

I've killed Tim.

I sprint across 209 and ineffectually drag my bulk around Industrial Grotto, weeping and banging on locked corporate doors. United Knee Wrap's having a gala. Their top brass are drunkenly lip-synching hits of the fifties en masse and their foot soldiers are laughing like subservient fools, so no one hears my frantic knocking. I prepare to heave a fake boulder through the plate glass. But then I stop. By now Tim's beyond help. What do I gain by turning myself in? Did I or did I not save an innocent girl's life? Was he or was he not a cruel monster? What's done is done. My peace of mind is gone forever. Why spend the remainder of my life in jail for the crime of eliminating a piece of filth?

And standing there outside the gala I learn something vital about myself: when push comes to shove, I could care less about lofty ideals. It's me I love. It's me I want to protect.

Me.

I hustle back to the office for the burial gear. I roll Tim into the pit. I sprinkle on lime and cover him with dirt. I forge a letter in which he claims to be going to Mexico to clarify his relationship with God via silent meditation in a rugged desert setting.

"My friends," I write through tears in his childish scrawl, 'you slave away for minimal rewards! Freedom can be yours if you open yourself to the eternal! Good health and happiness to you all. I'm truly sorry for any offense I may have given. Especially to you, Freeda, who deserved a better man than the swine I was. I am a new man now, and Freeda dear, I suggest counseling. Also: I have thought long and hard on this, and have decided to turn over the reins to Jeffrey, whom I have always wrongly maligned. I see now that he is a man of considerable gifts, and ask you all to defer to him as you would to me."

I leave the letter on Claude's chair and go out to sleep in my car. I dream of Tim wearing a white robe in a Mexican cantina. A mangy dog sits on his lap explaining the rules of the dead. No weeping. No pushing the other dead. Don't bore everyone with tales of how great you were. Tim smiles sweetly and rubs the dog behind the ears. He sees me and says no hard feelings and thanks for speeding him on to the realm of bliss.

I wake with a start. The sun comes up, driving sparrows before it, turning the corporate reflective windows wild with orange. I roll out of my car and brush my teeth with my finger.

My first day as a killer.

I walk to the pit in the light of fresh day, hoping it was all a dream. But no. There's our scuffling footprints. There's the mound of fresh dirt, under which lies Tim. I sit on a paint can in a patch of waving weeds and watch my colleagues arrive. I weep. I think sadly of the kindly bumbler I used to be, bleary-eyed in the morning, guiltless and looking forward to coffee.

When I finally go in, everyone's gathered stunned around the microwave.

"El Presidente," Claude says disgustedly.

"Sorry?" I say.

I make a big show of shaking my head in shock as I read and reread the note I wrote. I ask if this means I'm in charge. Claude says with that kind of conceptual grasp we're not exactly in for salad days. He asks Freeda if she had an inkling. She says she always knew Tim had certain unplumbed depths but this is ridiculous. Claude says he smells a rat. He says Tim never had a religious bone in his body and didn't speak a word of Spanish. My face gets red. Thank God Blamphin, that toady, pipes up.

"I say in terms of giving Jeffrey a chance, we should give Jeffrey a chance, inasmuch as Tim was a good manager but a kind of a mean guy," he says.

"Well put," Claude says cynically. "And I say this fattie knows something he's not telling."

I praise Tim to the skies and admit I could never fill his shoes. I demean my organizational skills and leadership abilities but vow to work hard for the good of all. Then I humbly propose a vote: Do I assume leadership or not? Claude says he'll honor a quorum, and then via show of hands I achieve a nice one.

I move my things into Tim's office. Because he'd always perceived me as a hefty milquetoast with no personal aspirations, he trusted me implicitly. So I'm able to access the corporate safe. I'm able to cater in prime rib and a trio of mustachioed violinists, who stroll from cubicle to cubicle hoping for tips. Claude's outraged. Standing on his chair, he demands to know whatever happened to the profit motive. Everyone ignores him while munching on my prime rib and enjoying my musicians. He says one can't run a corporation on good intentions and blatant naïveté. He pleads that the staff fire me and appoint him CEO. Finally Blamphin proposes I can him. Torson from Personnel seconds the motion. I shrug my shoulders and we vote, and Claude's axed. He kicks the watercooler. He gives me the finger. But out he goes, leaving us to our chocolate mousse and cocktails.

By nightfall the party's kicked into high gear. I bring in jugglers and a comedian and drinks, drinks, drinks. My staff swears their undying loyalty. We make drunken toasts to my health and theirs. I tell them we'll kill no more. I tell them we'll come clean with the appropriate agencies and pay all relevant fines. Henceforth we'll relocate the captured raccoons as we've always claimed to be doing. The company will be owned by us, the employees, who will come and go as we please. Beverages and snacks will be continually on hand. Insurance will be gratis. Day care will be available on-site.

Freeda brightens and sits on the arm of my chair.

Muzak will give way to personal steros in each cubicle. We will support righteous charities, take troubled children under our collective wing, enjoy afternoons off when the sun is high and the air sweet with the smell of mown grass, treat one another as family, send one another fond regards on a newly installed electronic mail system, and, when one of us finally has to die, we will have the consolation of knowing that, aided by corporate largesse, our departed colleague has known his or her full measure of power, love, and beauty, and arm in arm we will all march to the graveyard, singing sad hymns.

Just then the cops break in, led by Claude, who's holding one of Tim's shoes.

"If you went to Mexico," he shouts triumphantly, "wouldn't you take your Porsche? Would you be so stupid as to turn your life's work over to this tub of lard? Things started to add up. I did some literal digging. And there I found my friend Tim, with a crushed rib cage that broke my heart, and a look of total surprise on his face."

"My Timmy," Freeda says, rising from my chair. "This disgusting pig killed my beautiful boy."

They cuff me and lead me away.

In court I tell the truth. The animal rights girl comes out of the woodwork and corroborates my story. The judge says he appreciates my honesty and the fact that I saved a life. He wonders why having saved the life, I didn't simply release Tim and reap the laurels of my courage. I tell him I lost control. I tell him a lifetime of scorn boiled over. He says he empathizes completely. He says he had a weight problem himself when a lad.

Then he gives me fifty as opposed to life without parole.

So now I know misery. I know the acute discomfort of a gray jail suit pieced together from two garments of normal size. I know the body odor of Vic, a Chicago kingpin who's claimed me for his own and compels me to wear a feminine hat with fruit on the brim for nightly interludes. Do my ex-colleagues write? No. Does Freeda? Ha. Have I achieved serenity? No. Have I transcended my horrid surroundings and thereby won the begrudging admiration of my fellow cons? No. They exult in hooting at me nude during group showers. They steal my allotted food portions. Do I have a meaningful hobby that makes the days fly by like minutes? No. I have a wild desire to smell the ocean. I have a sense that God is unfair and preferentially punishes his weak, his dumb, his fat, his lazy. I believe he takes more pleasure in his perfect creatures, and cheers them on like a brainless dad as they run roughshod over the rest of us. He gives us a need for love, and no way to get any. He gives us a desire to be liked, and personal attributes that make us utterly unlikable. Having placed his flawed and needy children in a world of exacting specifications, he deducts the difference between what we have and what we need from our hearts and our self-esteem and our mental health.

This is how I feel. These things seem to me true. But what's there to do but behave with dignity? Keep a nice cell. Be polite but firm when Vic asks me to shimmy while wearing the hat. Say a kind word when I can to the legless man doing life, who's perennially on toilet duty. Join in at the top of my lungs when the geriatric murderer from Baton Rouge begins his nightly spiritual.

Maybe the God we see, the God who calls the daily shots, is merely a subGod. Maybe there's a God above this subGod, who's busy for a few Godminutes with something else, and will be right back, and when he gets back will take the subGod by the ear and say, "Now look. Look at that fat man. What did he ever do to you? Wasn't he humble enough? Didn't he endure enough abuse for a thousand men? Weren't the simplest tasks hard? Didn't you sense him craving affection? Were you unaware that his days unraveled as one long bad dream?" And maybe as the subGod slinks away, the true God will sweep me up in his arms, saying: My sincere apologies, a mistake has been made. Accept a new birth, as token of my esteem.

And I will emerge again from between the legs of my mother, a slighter and more beautiful baby, destined for a different life, in which I am masterful, sleek as a deer, a winner.

Offloading for Mrs. Schwartz

ELIZABETH ALWAYS THOUGHT the fake stream running through our complex was tacky. Whenever I'd sit brooding beside it after one of our fights she'd hoot down at me from the balcony. Then I'd come in and we'd make up. Oh would we. I think of it. I think of it and think of it. Finally in despair I call GuiltMasters. GuiltMasters are Jean and Bob Fleen, a brother/sister psychiatric practice. In their late-night TV ads they wear cowls and capes and stand on either side of a sobbing neurotic woman in sweater and slacks. By the end of the bit she's romping through a field of daisies. I get Jean Fleen. I tell her I've done a bad thing I can't live with. She says I've called the right place. She says there's nothing so shameful it can't be addressed by GuiltMasters. I take a deep breath and spill my guts. There's a silence from Jean's end. Then she asks can I hold. Upbeat Muzak comes on. Several minutes later Bob comes on and asks can they call me back. I wait by the phone. One hour, two hours, all night. Nothing. The sun comes up. Brad from Complex Grounds turns on the bubbler and the whitewater begins to flow. I don't shower. I don't shave. I put on the same pants I had on before. It's too much. Three years since her death and still I'm a wreck. I think of fleeing the city. I think of working on a shrimper, or setting myself on fire downtown.

Instead I go to work.

In spite of my problems, personal interactive holography marches on.

All morning I hopefully dust. Nobody comes in. At noon I work out a little tension by running amok in one of my modules. I choose Bowling with the Pros. A holographic smoothie in a blazer greets me and affably asks if I'm as tired as he is of perennially overhooking the ball when what I really need is to consistently throw strikes. I tell him fuck off. In a more sophisticated module he'd ask why the hostility, but my equipment is outdated and instead he looks confused and tries to shake my hand. What crappy verisimilitude. No wonder I'm in the red. No wonder my rent's overdue. He asks isn't bowling a lovely recreation? I tell him I'm in mourning. He says the hours spent in a bowling alley with friends certainly make for some fantastic memories years down the line. I tell him my life's in the crapper. He grins and says let's bowl, let's go in and bowl, let's go in and bowl a few frames – with the Pros! I take him by the throat. Of course he Dysfunctions. Of course I'm automatically unbooted. I doff my headset and dismount the treadmill. Once again it's just me and my failing shop. Once again the air reeks of microwaved popcorn. Once again I am only who I am.

Wonderful, I think, you've fouled your own four-hundred-dollar module. And I have. So I trash it. I write it off to grief management. I go to lunch. I opt for an autodispensed FreightFurter. Of course I overmicrowave and the paper cowcatcher melds with the bun and the little engineer's face runs down his overalls. It's even more inedible than usual. I chuck it. I can't afford another. I chuck it and go wait for my regulars.

At two Mr. Bomphil comes in looking guilty and as always requests Violated Prom Queen, then puts on high heels and selects Treadmill Three. Treadmill Three is behind a beam, so he's free to get as worked up as he likes, which is very. I try not to hear him moan. I try not to hear him call each football-team member by name. He's followed by Theo Kiley, an appliance salesman who lays down a ream of Frigidaire specs and asks for Legendary American Killers Stalk You. I strap on his headset. I insert his module. For twenty minutes he hems and haws with Clyde Barrow. Finally he slips up and succumbs to a burst of machine-gun fire, then treats himself to a Sprite. "Whew," he says. "Next time I'll know to avoid the topic of his mom." I remind him he's got an outstanding bill. He says thanks. He says his bill and his ability to match wits with great criminals are the only outstanding things he's got. We laugh. We laugh some more. He shakes his head and leaves. I curse him under my breath, then close up early and return to my lonely home.

NEXT DAY MRS. GAITHER from Corporate comes to town. Midway through my Significant Accomplishments Assessment, armless Mr. Feltriggi comes to the door and as usual rings the bell with his face. I let him in and he unloads his totebag of cookbooks for sale. Today its "Crazy Cajun Carnival" and "Going Bananas with Bananas: A Caribbean Primer." But I know what he really wants. With my eyes I tell him wait. Finally Gaither finishes raking my sub-par Disbursement Ledger over the coals and goes across the mall to O My God for some vintage religious statuary. I slip the headset on Feltriggi and run Youth Roams Kansas Hometown, 1932. It's all homemade bread and dirt roads and affable dogcatchers. What a sweet grin appears. He greets each hometowner with his ghost limbs and beams at the chirping of the holographic birds. He kneels awhile in Mrs. Lawler's larder, sniffing spices that remind him of his

61

mother elbow-deep in flour. He drifts out to the shaded yard and discusses Fascism with the iceman near some swaying wheat. His posture changes for the better. He laughs aloud. He's young again and the thresher has yet to claim his arms.

Gaither comes back with a Saint Sebastian cookie jar. I nudge Feltriggi and tell him that's all for today. I take off his headset and he offers me a cookbook in payment. I tell him forget it. I tell him that's what friends are for. It's seventy bucks a session and he knows it. He rams his head into my chest as a sign of affection.

"That type of a presence surely acts to deflate revenues," Gaither says primly as Feltriggi goes out.

"No lie," I say. "That's why I nearly beat him up every time he comes in here."

"I'm not sure that's appropriate," she says.

"Me neither," I say. "That's why I usually don't really do it."

"I see," she says. "Let's talk briefly about personal tragedy. No one's immune. But at what point must mourning cease? In your case, apparently never."

I think: You never saw Elizabeth lanky and tan and laughing in Napa.

"I like your cookie jar," I say.

"Very well," she says, "seal your own doom."

She says she's shocked at the dryness of my treadmill bearings and asks if I've ever heard of oil. She sighs and gives me her number at the Quality Inn in case I think of anything that might argue against Franchise Agreement Cancellation. Then out she goes, sadly shaking her head.

It's only my livelihood. It's only every cent Elizabeth left me. I load up my mobile pack. I select my happiest modules. Then I go off to my real job, my penance, my albatross.

*

ROCKETTOWN'S OUR GHETTO. It's called Rockettown because long ago they put up a building there in which to build rockets. But none were built and the building's now nothing, which is what it's always been, except for a fenced-off dank corner that was once used to store dilapidated fireplugs and is now a filthy day-care for the children of parents who could care less. All around Rockettown little houses went up when it was thought the building would soon be full of people making rockets and hauling down impressive wages. They're bad little houses, put up quick, and now all the people who were young and had hoped to build rockets are old and doddering and walk by the empty building mumbling why why why.

In the early days of my grief Father Luther told me to lose myself in service by contacting Elder Aid, Inc. I got Mrs. Ken Schwartz. Mrs. Ken Schwartz lives in Rockettown. She lives in Rockettown remembering Mr. Ken Schwartz and cursing him for staying so late at Menlo's TenPin on nights when she forgets he's been dead eighteen years. Mrs. Ken Schwartz likes me and my happy modules. Especially she likes Viennese Waltz. Boy does she. She's bedridden and lonely and sometimes in her excitement bruises her arms on her headboard when the orchestra starts to play. Tonight she says she's feeling weak. She says she used to be a different person and wishes she could go back to the days when she was loved. She mourns Fat Patrice and their jovial games of Old Maid. She mourns the front-yard oak the city felled without asking her. Mostly she mourns Mr. Ken Schwartz.

I pull out all the stops. I set Color on high contrast. I tape sensors to her lips and earlobes. I activate the Royalty Subroutine. Soon the prince is lavishing her with praise. Soon they're sneaking off from the ball for some tender words and

63

a kiss or two on a stone bench beside the Danube. Soon I'm daubing her eyes with tissue while she weeps at the beauty of the fishermen bowing from their little boats as they realize it's the prince himself trying to retrieve her corsage from the river.

I make tea. I read my magazine. Finally I stroke her forehead while humming Strauss and slowly fading the volume.

"You,' she says, smiling sweetly when she's all the way back. "You're too good to me."

"No one could be too good to you,' I say.

"Oh you,' she says. "You're a saint."

No, I think, I'm a man without a life, due to you. Then I feel ashamed and purposely bash my shin against the bedframe while tucking her in. I get her some juice. I check her backdoor lock. All around the room are dirty plates I've failed to get to the sink and old photos of Mr. Ken Schwartz assessing the condition of massive steamboilers while laughing confidently.

Out on the street it's cold and a wino's standing in a Dumpster calling a stray cat Uncle Chuck. I hustle directly to my Omni, fearing for my gear. I drive through frightening quarters of the city, nervously toggling my defrost lever, thinking of Mrs. Schwartz. The last few months she's gone downhill. She's unable to feed herself or autonomously use the bathroom. Talk about losing yourself in service to a greater extent than planned. She needs a live-in, but they don't come cheap, and my shop hasn't turned a profit in months. What to do? I think and think. I think so much I lose track of where I am and blunder by The Spot. You fool, I think, you ass, how much additional pain would you like? Here a drunk named Tom Clifton brought his Coupe De Ville onto the sidewalk as Elizabeth shopped for fruit on the evening of a day when we'd fought like hell. On the evening of a day when I'd called her an awful name. What name? I can't say the word. I even think it and my gut burns.

I'm a saint.

The fight started when I accused her of flirting with our neighbor Len Kobb by bending low on purpose. I was angry and implied that she couldn't keep her boobs in her top to save her life. If I could see her one last time I'd say: Thanks very much for dying at the worst possible moment and leaving me holding the bag of guilt. I'd say: If you had to die, couldn't you have done it when we were getting along?

I madly flee The Spot. There are boat lights in the harbor and a man in a tux inexplicably jogging through the park. There's a moon bobbing up between condemned buildings. There's the fact that tomorrow I'm Lay Authority Guest at the Lyndon Baines Johnson School for Precocious Youth. I'm slated to allow interested kids to experience the module entitled Hop-Hop the Bunny Masters Fractions. Frankly I fear I'll be sneered at. How interested could a mob of gifted kids be in a rabbit and a lisping caterpillar grouping acorns ad nauseam? But I've promised the principal, Mrs. Briff. And I'm not in a position to decline any revenue source. So at an hour of the night when other men my age are rising from their beds to comfort screaming newborns I return to the mall for my Hop-Hop module.

I use my passkey. Something's strange. Modules are strewn everywhere. The cashbox sits on the fax machine. One of my treadmills lies on its side.

"How is all of this fancy equipment used?" someone asks from behind me, pressing a sharp knife to my throat. "More specifically, which of it is worth the most? And remember, sir, you're answering for your life."

He sounds old but feels strong. I tell him it's hard to explain. I offer to demonstrate. He says do so, but slowly. I

65

fit him with a headset. I gently guide him to a treadmill, then run Sexy Nurses Scrub You Down. Immediately his lips get moist. Immediately he pops a mild bone and loosens his grip on the knife and I'm able to coldcock him with the FedEx tape gun. He drops drooling to my nice carpet. A man his age should be a doting grandfather, not a crook threatening me with death. I feel violated. How does someone come to this?

I strap him down and set my console for Scan.

It seems his lousy name is Hank. I hear his portly father calling it out across a cranberry bog. I know the smell of his first baseball cap. Through his eyes I see the secret place under the porch where he hid whenever his fat kissing aunt came. Later I develop a love for swing. It seems he was a Marine at Iwo who on his way to boot camp saw the aging Ty Cobb at a depot. I sense his panic on the troop transport, then quickly doff my headset as he hits the beach and the bullets start to fly.

To my horror, I see that his eyelids are fluttering and his face is contorting. My God, I think, this is no Scan, this is a damn Offload. I check the console. Sure enough, via one incorrect switch setting, I've just irrevocably transferred a good third of his memories to my hard drive.

He comes to and hops off the table looking years younger, suddenly happy-go-lucky, asks where he is, and trots blithely out the door, free now of boot camp, free of Iwo, free of all memory of youthful slaughter, free in fact of any memory at all of the first twenty years of his life. I'm heartsick. What have I done? On the other hand, it stopped him from getting up and trying to kill me. On the other hand, it appears he left here a happier man, perhaps less inclined to felony.

I grab my Hop-Hop module. On the cover is Hop-Hop, enthusiastically giving the thumbs-up to an idealized blond boy lifting an enormous 4 into a numerator. As if being robbed weren't enough, first thing tomorrow morning a roomful of genius kids is going to eat me alive.

Then, crossing the deserted Food Court, I get a brainstorm.

I hustle back to the shop and edit out Hank's trysts with starving women in Depression-era hobo camps and his one homo fling with his cousin Julian. I edit the profanity out of Iwo. I edit out the midnight wanks, the petty thefts, the un-kind words, all but the most inoffensive of the bodies of his buddies on the pale sand beach.

Next morning I herd kid after kid behind my white curtain and let them experience Hank's life. They love it. They leave jabbering knowledgeably about the Pacific Theater and the ultimate wisdom of using the Bomb. They leave humming "American Patrol." They leave praising Phil Rizzuto's field-ing and cursing the Brown Shirts. They pat old Mr. Panchuko, the geriatric janitor, on the back and ask him what caliber machine gun he operated at the Bulge. He stands scratching his gut, stunned, trying to remember. The little Klotchkow twins jitterbug. Andy Pitlin, all of three feet tall, hankers aloud for a Camel.

Mrs. Briff is more than impressed. She asks what else I have. I ask what else does she want. She says for starters how about the remainder of the century. I tell her I'll see what I can do.

The kids come out of it with a firsthand War Years experience and I come out of it with a check for five hun-dred dollars, enough to hire a temporary live-in for Mrs. Ken Schwartz. Which I gladly do. A lovely Eurasian named Wei, a student of astrophysics, who, as I'm leaving them alone for the first time, is brushing out Mrs. Ken Schwartz's hair and humming "Let Me Call You Sweetheart."

"Will you stay forever?" I ask her.

"With all due respect," she replies, "I will stay as long as you can pay me."

TWO WEEKS LATER, Briff's on my tail for more modules and Wei's on my tail for her pay. I tell Mrs. Ken Schwartz all, during one of her fifteen-minute windows of lucidity. When lucid she's shrewd and bright. She understands her predicament. She understands the limitations of my gear. She understands that I can't borrow her memories, only take them away forever.

She says she can live without the sixties.

I haul my stuff over to her place and take what I need. I edit out her mastectomy, Ken Schwartz's midlife crisis and resulting trip to Florida, and her constant drinking in his absence. I stick to her walking past a protest and counseling a skinny girl on acid to stay in school. It's not great but I've got a deadline. I call it America in Tumult—The Older Generation Looks On in Dismay.

I have it couriered over to Briff, dreading her response. But to my amazement she sends a cash bonus. She reports astounding increases in grandparental bonding. She reports kids identifying a Mercury Cougar with no prompting and disgustedly calling each other Nixon whenever a trust is betrayed.

Thereafter I retain Wei on a weekly basis by whittling away at Mrs. Schwartz's memories. I submit Pearl Harbor—Week Prior to Infamy. I submit The Day the Music Died—Buddy Holly Remembered, which unfortunately is merely Mrs. Schwartz hearing the news on a pink radio, then disinterestedly going back to cleaning her oven. Finally Briff calls, hacked off. She says she wants some real meat. She asks how about the entire twenties, a personal favorite of hers. She's talking flappers. She's talking possible insights on Prohibition. I stonewall. I tell her give me a few days to exhaustively check my massive archive. I call Mrs. Ken Schwartz. She says during the twenties she was a lowly phone operator in Pekin, Illinois. She sounds disoriented, and wearily asks where her breasts are.

Clearly this has gone far enough.

I call Briff and tell her no more modules. She ups her offer to three thousand a decade. She's running for school board and says my modules are the primary arrow in her quiver. But what am I supposed to do? Turn Mrs. Schwartz into a well-cared-for blank slate? Start kidnapping and off-loading strangers? I say a little prayer: God, I've botched this life but good. I've failed you in all major ways. You gave me true love and I blew it. I'm nothing. But what have you got against Mrs. Ken Schwartz? Forgive me. Help me figure this out.

And then in a flash I figure it out.

I lock the shop. On the spine of a blank module I write 1951–1992—Baby Boomers Come Into Their Own. At three thousand a decade, that's twelve grand. I address an envelope to Briff and enclose an invoice. I write out some instructions and rig myself up.

Memories shmemories, I think, I'll get some new ones. These old ones give me no peace.

Then I let it rip. It all goes whizzing by: Anthony Newburg smacking me. Mom on the dock. An Agnew Halloween mask at a frat house. Bev Alalloy struggling with my belt. The many seasons. The many flags, dogs, paths, the many stars in skies of many hues.

My sweet Elizabeth.

Holding hands we gape at an elk in Estes Park. On our knees in a bed of tulips I kiss her cheek. The cold clear water of Nacogdoches. The birthday banner she made of scarves in our little place on Ellington. The awful look on her face as I

69

called her what I called her. Her hair, trailing fine and light behind her as she stormed out to buy fruit.

The grave, the grave, my sad attempt to become a franchise.

Then I'm a paunchy guy in a room, with a note pinned to his sleeve:

"You were alone in the world," it says, "and did a kindness for someone in need. Good for you. Now post this module, and follow this map to the home of Mrs. Ken Schwartz. Care for her with some big money that will come in the mail. Find someone to love. Your heart has never been broken. You've never done anything unforgivable or hurt anyone beyond reparation. Everyone you've ever loved you've treated like gold."

Downtrodden Mary's
Failed Campaign of Terror

M Y FIRST AND favorite task of the day is slaving over
the Iliana Evermore Fairy Castle. It's lovely. I turn
the Maintenance lights off and the fake stars come on
automatically. There's a short in the full moon over the
Fire Door, but unfortunately my Recommendations for
Corrective Action have been consistently ignored. I dust
all the furniture and remake the tiny four-poster, then add
colorant to the brook and wax the ballroom floor. I pick
lint off the fur items, such as the mouse rug with the teeth
still intact and the royal robe contributed by the Peruvian
ambassador in the Theodore Roosevelt days. I'm arranging
the tiny knights so they appear to be fording the stream
when the door flies open and the kids from the most slovenly day-care in the world come screaming in.

Every morning four minivans pull up and eighty kids pile
out and one supervising adult with a magazine. All day long
the kids run wild, indiscriminately pushing the interactive
exhibit buttons. Today a group of them surround me and ask
why I'm wearing a nightgown. I tell them it's no nightgown,
it's a frock. One cute little fellow says the hell it is. A little girl
calls me Grandma and asks if she can try on my wing harness

and I say certainly. The minute she gets it on, however, she makes an obscene gesture and runs off. Those wings are fifteen dollars to replace. I can't afford that. I'm old and stiff but finally I get her cornered near the Audio Enhancement Module. Just as I get my hands on my wings the supervising adult comes rushing up and says how dare I hamper the child's self-esteem by being critical of her impulses? She tells the little girl that if she takes the wings out into the hall she'll be free to explore and grow as she sees fit. Then she stands in my path and glares at me.

An hour later the children have left and my wings have not been returned.

So I go down to Administration to break the news to Mr. Spencer, Cleaning Coordinator, praying in my heart for a time-deferred payroll deduction.

ON HIS OFFICE wall Mr. Spencer has nine watercolors of the space shuttle and a photograph of himself crying the day the *Challenger* crashed. He says because he's in a good mood he'll give me two weeks to pay for the wings before firing me. Then he asks do I want to know why he's so happy. I don't but I say I do. He says he's so happy because while he was on vacation the see-through cow didn't die. Spread across his desk are photos of the cow for his upcoming poster session. The see-through cow is his main career asset. Via the cow he hopes to get out of Cleaning and into Curation. Mr. Jorgsen in Applied Biology did the theoretical calculations proving the cow was possible, but he never intended anyone to actually implement. Mr. Spencer got hold of the plans and through slander had Jorgsen demoted to Exhibit Repair. The great scandal the public doesn't know about however is that the cows don't last. We've been through six already. It's very hush-hush. When one dies, a special team comes in and alters the new cow to look like the original, using special fur makeup. Then the surgical group whisks it away and implants a Plexiglas window in its flank.

Mr. Spencer has me listen to his presentation. It concerns ingestion-to-defecation ratios and problems experienced with the flesh/window junction. He throws in a few cow one-liners that are not effective. Of course he doesn't mention the deaths. When he's done I tell him it was excellent and he reminds me to subtract the time spent listening to him from my time sheet so I don't inadvertently get paid for it.

I get up to leave and he asks what's next on my agenda. I say Break. He says not so fast, then orders me to clean up some vomit from near the Pickled Babies. I ask him please no. Three stillborns was my lot and the Pickled Babies first thing in the morning is too much.

But he cheerfully recites the Employee Loyalty Oath and says he's not in the mood to negotiate and tells me to please shake a leg for Christ's sake.

ON THE WAY to the Pickled Babies I pass poor Mr. Jorgsen standing forlorn in the railroad diorama. The church comes up to his knees and he's losing his mind. He feels bad for having designed the see-through cow. Of late he's been kicking the diorama apart, and the scuttlebutt is he's one building away from dismissal. I say good morning and he sits down disconsolately on Mount Hood. At the Nutritional Evaluation Module several teenage members of Special Duties are estimating their percentage bodyfat by typing information in on a giant lettuce head. I say hello and they look over at me meanly.

The world has certainly changed since I was a girl.

At ninety-two years old people assume you're dense. They assume you don't remember being young and have corny moral values and can't hear well. But oh how I remember sex with Herb, the one good man I've known. He played a beautiful soft guitar. We met at a fruit stand. How we experimented in his trailer before my husband Bud and his repulsive gangster friends slit his throat and dumped him off a barge into the CalSag. After killing Herb the lot of them came over to our place for dinner as usual. Oh I was beside myself. All of them had excellent appetites. Every Sunday they came. After eating they would take their shirts off and talk gangster strategy in the front room. I would do the dishes and sit on the porch in hopes they would forget about me. But invariably Bud would have me try on a dress for the group. The day he killed Herb he made me put on a cigarette-girl get-up and serve dessert out of it bending low.

Perhaps I should have put up more of a fight but after what happened to my brother I was never one to rock the boat. He was a Wobbly and went out West, where they cut off his penis and hung him from a bridge. And did you know they shipped him back without cleaning him up one bit and my poor mother had to view the body of her only son without its penis and with such a horrible rope burn on the neck?

She was never the same. We were continually finding dead chicks about the house.

And that is why I moved to the city.

That is why I moved to the city and before long was married to a man with all gold teeth, who used them to bite painful arcs into my legs. Bud was brutal through and through. A young girl gets extremely worked up on the honeymoon and the next thing she knows her new husband is scampering into the kitchen for a zucchini squash. Even through my crying he insisted, saying it would bring us closer together. Imagine the humiliation of being just eighteen and having to go to your family doctor with an infection difficult to explain. Finally he found it in a plant book. That you don't live down. But what I've put up with I've put up with for what I thought at the time was love. What was I to do? Nowadays things may be different but in those days a woman had no place to go.

At the eighth of the nine display cases explaining about diesels my knees give out and I sit down next to an empty popcorn box on a marble bench. At my age, every time you sit down you fall asleep. When I wake up Mitzi's taking a photograph of me supine. She's Mr. Spencer's young tart. For months she's been shopping around for a doctor willing to surgically lengthen her legs. Mr. Spencer never asks her to clean vomit. He never asks her to do anything but you-know-what in a bunk in the captured Nazi sub.

She says: When Matt sees this shot he'll take you down to four an hour so fast it'll make your head spin.

Then she goes off, practicing a sexy way of walking.

I picture her hanging on the meathook Bud and company kept in their gangster clubhouse, then proceed down to The Wonder That Is Our Body.

THE PICKLED BABIES range in age from two weeks to full term. They float in green fluid in jars with black lids. Often in the Louis Pasteur Memorial Break Room we speculate on how they were obtained. I'm certain Dr. Cardilla would have had my stillborns disposed of in a Christian manner. Don't think I haven't closely inspected the face of the full-term. That poor fellow barely fits in his jar and the lid has made a flat place in his head but he looks nothing like me and nothing like Bud. How I remember Bud paying off Dr. Cardilla so I could hold each of them a few minutes longer. For all his horrible faults Bud made good money. He made good money doing odd jobs for the frightening Quinn brothers, such as killing a Chinese on our back lawn. I was making dinner when I witnessed that. When Bud fell asleep I snuck outside and looked at that poor Chinese in the moonlight. One leg was pulled up and his hands were in fists. The next morning when I went out to cut lilacs he was gone. I believe Tom Quinn took him away in his milk truck.

Of course not a cent of Bud's money is left, because I was bilked by a nice boy claiming to be a Mormon. He'd certainly done his homework by studying the Charleston. We danced it for hours. He was no more Mormon than the man in the moon. What a fool I was. He brought his children over and I made them cookies shaped like their hands, using wax paper and a color crayon. I gave him my savings and for several months he sent me photos of a ski resort he said we owned together, and then he sent me one last photo, of himself naked atop a young woman in a steam-bath. That I feel was the crudest part. That and a very filthy letter.

He seemed so nice.

As I approach the Babies I see that the vomit is the least of my worries. Six Months, Eleven Days has been knocked from his shelf. His jar is broken and a stream of formaldehyde is running towards the escalator.

Mr. Spencer comes around the corner with a Trustee and at the top of his lungs demands to know why I'm not wearing protective gloves. For a second I think he's being considerate of my health but then he explains to the Trustee that oil from my hands will discolor the baby and require its replacement.

Then he says: Sometimes I think I should insist on an age cut-off, this is like working with human vegetables.

They walk off and I think: All right for you buster.

I do what I can for that poor little dead child, then stop by my locker for the rat poison and proceed to Our Nation's Bounty to send another see-through cow to God.

*

76

OUR NATION'S BOUNTY is a far cry from a meadow. I was once a farm girl myself. When Father came in smelling of compost my sisters and I would run for the closet. He would either beat us or stroke us excessively. Still, when he died I was sad. Our Nation's Bounty has a barn façade and a few real tractors and a stuffed farmer but they've located it next to Riches from the Bowels of the Earth and in my opinion cows aren't stupid. What I mean is to say is, certainly they are stupid, but they have sound enough instincts to know that a functioning scaled-down coal mine with collegiate tour guides in hard hats is not part of any farm.

The cow looks up at me kindly as I come in.

I kneel down and pretend to Windex her panel. Inside there's plenty of activity. The idea was to provide schoolchildren insight into the digestive process of a large mammal. They claim the dyes aren't toxic. I would think however that the flesh/Plexiglas junction must be a source of constant irritation. But compassion is not why I've killed six to date. I've killed them because I like to make Mr. Spencer sad. Because of me he's pinned down in Cleaning, and Curation is out of the question. Because of me the see-through cow is a boondoggle and a white elephant and Spencer is a laughingstock.

It feels good to finally be asserting oneself.

They must put artificial flavoring in the rat poison because every cow so far has gulped it down like candy. This one does too, while whipping around its tan tail. She swallows the last of the batch, then turns her head towards the geodesic dome and begins foaming at the mouth.

As fast as I can, which I admit isn't very fast, I race down to the basement and take my break.

Within the hour Mr. O'Connell the cow contractor comes in with his briefcase, looking glad. Whenever a new cow comes in, he drives it through downtown in a pickup. Lawyers and businessmen sprint down the curb, shouting sayings at it. The cows arrive disoriented and nervous, then go in for surgery.

As he walks past he admits to no one in particular that for him the last few months have been salad days. Then he joins Mr. Spencer and they take the transparent elevator alongside the Foucault Pendulum up to where the cow is by now I would imagine lying with stiff legs. Mr. Spencer is pounding his fist into his palm and saying he suspects sabotage and Mr. O'Connell is trying hard not to look jubilant.

I start to worry. I go down to the Fairy Castle. It s time for the daily blizzard. Two young black men climb into the rafters to refill the bags, and the snow starts to fall. It's so restful and nice until Mr. Spencer comes in with all nine Trustees. He holds out my last pack of poison and asks how could I, then he hastens to add that locker spot-checks are fully legal.

He takes me by the collar and marches me out to the front door, through Photos to Bring Back Memories of a Lifetime and the Gallery of Astounding Communications. All along the way the Trustees talk in low tones about senility. We pass Mr. Jorgsen, who salutes me and starts singing the "Marseillaise." Beneath the Flags of All Nations Mr. Spencer calls me a criminal and shoves me roughly out into the cold, and will not even allow me to fetch my coat. I walk down the umpteen stairs, my knees burning like hot coals. My ankles hurt and my piles hurt and the wind from the lake is stinging my cataracts. From the revolving door Mr. Spencer shouts that he hopes God will forgive me, and the Trustees applaud him.

In the plain blue day is my city, the city where I lived, the city that, in my own fashion, I loved. I remember when it was made entirely of wood, and men sold goods from carts, and this museum was a floodplain where we all picnicked.

I dodder shivering out along the cold cold pier, surrounded by staring Navy boys. The air smells of their hair tonic, and golden dead fish are bobbing in huge numbers against the chicken wire. I think of how lovely it all could have been had anything gone right, and then I think: Oh heavens, why prolong it, I've no income now.

I step off the pier, followed by nine or ten of the Navy boys, who want to save me, and do, and will not stop saving me although I beg and beg and beg. They deposit me on the frozen sand and cover me with their coats, and walk around patting each other on the back and shouting with triumph.

One has a radio and they begin to dance.

Bounty

Tonight at last the nation votes. In defiance of top management Father Oswald's set up his shortwave in the Rec Center. He says no matter how the vote turns out we've got to buck up. He says no matter what happens we've been blessed. Though it's true, he admits, that our burdens are considerable crosses to bear, we still get three squares a day, not to mention a nice chunk of change to take home and mull over in the privacy and security of a bunkhouse for which we pay zippo rent.

We try to go through our regular Counseling agenda. We talk about ways in which we feel neglected or trampled underfoot. We pair off and exchange neckrubs while praising one another for being so unique. Then Father leads us in cheerful songs from musicals. But nobody can concentrate. Finally he gives in and turns on the news: Poll riots in Cleveland and three Flaweds lynched outside Topeka. The early returns are discouraging. The Western vote will decide it. Out there genetic purity is highly valued and Flaweds are generally considered subhuman trash, so things look bleak.

Father gathers us around him in a circle and encourages us to visualize losing so that when we actually do it won't hurt so much. Then he chucks each of us on the temple and says he's proud of our restraint.

By midnight it's clear we've lost. In spite of our Preemptive Visualization we're devastated. Beatrice Connally falls on the floor weeping. She's forty-two and sees the vote as a death knell for her baby hopes. Her wig goes askew and we can all see her huge scalp veins.

Father climbs up on a folding chair and gives us his The World Has Changed But Not Christ speech. He reminds us that what tortures us is desire. He suggests we take what comes and avail ourselves of the beauties present even in our reduced circumstances. Instead of having children, he says, plant and savor flowers. Instead of owning property, say a kind word to a neighbor with poor self-esteem.

"Bear in mind," he says, "that in time you meek shall inherit the earth."

"How can you possibly believe that line at a time like this?" Beatrice says from the floor, as several of her cronies hustle to get her wig back on.

"It is at times like these," he says, "that I believe most firmly."

"Easy for you to say," Beatrice says. "You're Normal."

"He's not normal," someone says. "He's a priest."

"No need for personal invective," Father says. "Although certainly I understand your frustrations."

Allan Burns makes a farting noise with his mouth from the back of the room. Allan's a cynical rebel with benign polyps all over his torso. He's nobody's favorite. Even sans polyps he'd be a pariah.

"In the best interests of all," Father says, seeming to enjoy ignoring Allan, "I suggest we go about our business as usual, observing the regular and sanctioned coping rituals."

The rest of us agree.

So he goes into the safe for our vials and we all toot up.

*

81

LATER THAT NIGHT in the Castle 4 courtyard Bill Tiney's screaming at a group of Clients for letting his son die of cholera. Little Scotty Tiney's lying motionless on a wooden cart near the goat-udder bagpipist. He's not really dead, he's Performing. Makeup's done a super job of making him look decayed. The Clients titter and check their Events Schedules and a few who are really in the spirit of the thing start laying coins on Scotty's chest. I'm slated for Ribald Highwayman. When the Tineys are through I'm supposed to bound in and rob the women of the fake jewelry they received at Admission, while comically ogling their cleavages.

Just then Connie comes up the trail with Mr. Corbett. I duck into a fake shrub. Connie's my sister. Corbett's a gigantic bachelor who made his fortune in antiseptic swabs.

"Say your husband's a burly peasant who'll kick my butt if I screw you," he says.

"My husband's a burly peasant who'll kick your butt if you screw me," Connie says.

"Wonderful," Mr. Corbett says. "Now fall down and let me catch up."

Connie pretends to trip. Corbett stands over her in his king's robe with his hands on his hips.

"You peasant girls," he says. "You peasant girls are all robust but naïve as to the ways of the world."

Lying there Connie scratches the side of her nose.

"Say my harsh words frighten you," Mr. Corbett says.

"Sire, your harsh words frighten me," Connie says.

"I like that," Mr. Corbett says. "I like that sire bit."

In violation of all specs I clip him in the neck with a rock. He just stands there looking stupid so I clip him again.

"I don't go for this," he says loudly.

So I clip him again.

"I'm not the kind of man who pays good money to be insulted," he says.

I clip him again and he makes a perturbed sound with his wet lips and stomps off. Connie gets up and looking out into the woods asks who's the smart-ass. She's mad because of the possible negative impact on her Performance Evaluation. But who cares. I'm still her brother. If she insists on having sex with rich guys for pay she can at least do it where I don't have to watch.

"I know it's you, Cole," she says. "If you love me, mind your own business."

Then she tromps back up the trail, cussing a blue streak and pleading with Corbett to come back and feel free to kick dirt on her. Meanwhile I've missed my cue by a mile. The courtyard's empty and the Clients are inside the castle making pigs of themselves while watching a troupe of Thespians bait an animatronic bear. I suspect my ass is in a sling. My experience has been that when the rich pay for Highwayman they expect damn Highwayman.

I go out to the retaining wall and climb into the guard station. Down in the tent town the dispossessed are having a hoedown. It's basically some floodlights mounted on gutted cars and pointed at a place where the dirt's been raked. For music they've got a fiddler and five or six earnest teens playing spoons. Some of the dispossessed kids are floating paper boats in our offal stream. It may be offal but in the moonlight it looks poignant enough.

After a while a few of the kids get bold and come skulking up to the wall. I search the guard station, then fling down some contingency dinner rolls. The kids squeal and fill their pockets and stand there yelling thanks and begging for more on the basis of how many infants they have at home.

Finally I shout down that I'm all out. They're sad about it and start back to the tent town with their crappy-looking shirts stuffed full of rolls.

"Smell one," one says as they go. "They smell so good."

The moon rises. The adult dispossessed wander off in pairs to their little shacks of packing material, as the fiddler stands on the hood of a car playing a sad good-night tune.

IN THE MORNING Mr. Oberlin wakes me by paging me in a stern tone. I go down to Administration and he's sitting at his desk with residual black bean soup on his lips. He eats the black bean every Tuesday to prove he's a man of the people. The black bean's an Employee staple. All day long the intrafacility PA touts its down-home hickory flavor. They don't have to sell us on it, since there's nothing else for us to eat. Mr. Albert's there too, wearing some kind of arts-and-crafts cardigan courtesy of his squeaky-clean wife. Albert's so stable and nice and generous he makes everyone uncomfortable. Oberlin points at a footstool with his nail file and says sit.

So I sit.

"Just for grins,' he says," paraphrase me our Statement of Corporate Mission."

"Give it your best try," Albert says kindly.

"To allow the deserving to experience an historical epoch unlike our own in terms of personal comfort," I read directly off their thirtieth-anniversary corporate ties.

"Whoa," Albert says. "Verbatim."

"Would you classify getting hit in the neck with a rock as experiencing comfort?" Oberlin says.

"I suppose what Mr. Oberlin's asking is," Albert says, "do you think that actual medieval royalty members were frequently hit in their necks with rocks?"

"Yes, my friend," Oberlin says, "the Corbett cat is out of the bag."

"Tell me," Albert says, scooting his chair close. "Was this a political reaction to last night's vote?"

"No," I say. "He was degrading my sister."

"Albeit with her permission," Albert says, handing me a mint. "We have her signed consent form."

"Another incident of this ilk and you may well find yourself wandering the wide world sans income my friend," Oberlin says. "And no joke. Bear in mind that in your case we're talking about a young man who was practically frigging born here, and who has apparently forgotten the considerable deprivations and pains-in-the-asses of existing without a potable water source, not to mention security from rampaging gangs that mean him harm."

"Wow," Albert says.

"In many senses," Oberlin says expansively, "I used to more or less like you in some ways. That's why I'm asking you to objectively regard your situation. Take off your shoes."

I give him a look.

"Just do it," he says.

So I take off my shoes. He sits next to me and takes off his.

"What I've got going here are toes," he says. "In your case, those may be fairly described as claws. Am I wrong?"

"No," I say. I could kill him for this. If there's one thing I'm well aware of it's the distinction between toes and claws.

"These feet identify you forever and always as Flawed," he says. "So even if you could somehow rid yourself of your Flawed bracelet, your deformed feet would scream out from every treetop the pertinent information on your unfortunate condition, by virtue of which, in the western portion of our nation, a man like yourself may literally be purchased and enslaved. Do I talk sense? Is this line of thought making a dent on your self-perception?"

"Yes," I say.

"Then why the offbeat actions?" he says. "Why the continual flying in the face of the hand that feeds you? One more chance, mother, and I'm going to put you on the road to knowledge of how lucky you truly are in your present employment circumstance. And don't think I won't."

Clearly he's threatening Expulsion. My stomach tightens. I try to look resolved and chastened and like I have a secret plan for corporate bravado. Out the window I see the McKremmer boys practicing their act on the Field of Battle by whacking each other with polyurethane jousting sticks while guffawing like idiots.

"And if you insist on sighing while I'm talking sense," Oberlin says, "that too will contribute to my overall assessment of you as some kind of squeaky wheel seeking grease. As for your sister, you yourself should strive to be such an admirable team player or noncomplaining spunky trooper. Which, *mon frère,* you are sadly not."

"And now for the bad news," Albert says.

"Inverse congratulations," Oberlin says. "You are hereby demoted to Table Boy."

"You've got to be kidding," I say.

"Company spirit, lad," Albert says. "It's the rudder on the otherwise wild boat of personal self-interest."

"Gleason party, Castle Two, three o'clock," Oberlin says. "Immerse yourself in your role. Try not to screw it up."

I can't believe it. Table Boy's the worst Assignment I've had since I was six and a Wandering Gypsy. Back then we'd approach some picnicking rich and Heloise Bremmer would start in on her sexy fortune-teller routine. Next came the Freaks, namely me and Brian Rumbley. Brian had an eye in the back of his head and would read Chaucer from a book I held behind him. In truth his third eye was a nonfunctional glutinous mass and he'd memorized the passage. Still it was effective. Then I'd do my dance. It's a hard dance to describe but it involved my claws and a sheet of plywood. Whenever she was mad at me Connie used to call it Tapping Without Tap Shoes. Because of my tender age the tips poured in. No one stopped to consider what the degradation might be doing to my psyche. At night Connie would sing me to sleep and tell me not to worry, because the real me was deep inside and safe. I love her dearly but in retrospect she had no idea what she was talking about. The real me was out there in tights, tripping the light fantastic for a bunch of soused rich vacationers. The real me was pining for my mother while showcasing my disability for a lousy buck.

Connie's lot was no better. At the time hayrides through the Peasant Village were all the rage. Her job was to run behind a horse named Maid Marian with a shovel and a plastic pail. The constant fecal contact made her sickly. Whenever she missed her poundage quota they made her scoop poop after dark. Then she fell for a Client, the Normal son of a transportation mogul. They met at the fake stream. He was having a smoke and reflecting on life and she was doing our laundry. By wearing baggy blouses over her bracelet she was able to deceive him into thinking she was Normal. For a week they snuck off into the woods and made big stupid promises. Then while touring with his parents he saw her hunched over a steaming mound with a look of concentration on her face and that was that. Her heart was broken. Shortly afterwards she started going wrong. I'd find her drunk and wandering along the moat in just a corset, shouting obscenities at members of Grounds.

And that was nothing compared to the going-wrong that followed.

If you want to feel depressed, try watching your only remaining family member go off into the woods for a romp with a trio of law enforcement bigwigs from Mahwah.

Connie's Flaw is a slight, very slight, vestigial tail. You can barely see it. After her jilting she went through a bad depression and tried to sand it off. She got a serious infection and was in the clinic for a week with compresses on her rear. When she came out she was humiliated and refused to speak. A week later she turned her first trick.

Sometimes I remember her at three years old on Easter morning, wearing a little coolie hat in the yard of the house on Marigold. We had a swing set. We had a bird feeder. We had a dog named Sparky. How we'd laugh as he'd caper around the yard digging at his anus with his mouth. When times got hard he was eaten against our will by our neighbor Mr. DeAngelo. Maybe it was for the best. A week later the militia took the house and we were driven out onto the road. Sparky would have been just one more mouth to feed. But still. Is it right that a couple of little kids should have to watch a grown overweight Italian man coldcock their father in order to bludgeon their dog to death with an eight-iron and roast it over an open fire? This was a man we'd seen swoon over a Christmas train set. This was a man who for laughs once ran through our sprinkler with a pair of underwear on his head. And there he was, weeping, dragging Sparky away by the paw. There he was, bellowing for his wife, cursing her for mislocating the Sterno cups, hacking up our pet with a cleaver in the shade of his bass boat. Who could forget his red-stained mouth? Who could forget him, satiated and contrite, offering Mom a shank?

Connie's a prostitute, I'm a thirty-year-old virgin, but all things considered, we could have turned out a lot worse.

I WALK PAST the beanfields and the Corporate Porcine Receptacle to cry on Connie's shoulder in the women's bunkhouse. The Receptacle is for the Dietary Supplement Pigs, hardened bits of which ultimately end up in the black bean soup. The Dietary Supplement Pigs are distinct from the Ambience Enhancement Pigs, which we breed special to resemble the coarse varieties extant during the actual Middle Ages, and whose primary function is to stand around the castle courtyard looking realistic.

The bunkhouse is empty. Then the lowly Ramirez twins come in from a morning of hand-lugging dirt clods in the beanfields. Connie considers Lupe and Maria a couple of excellent arguments for remaining a floozy. They're moral but not bright. They've got holy cards plastered all over their metal bedframes. They rarely speak and when they do are either proselytizing or claiming to have seen the Virgin Mary hovering above a moat. Last fall Mr. Oberlin suggested that Lupe might like to supplement her pay-check by spending sortie time in the Reward Suite with a high-school friend of his who'd done well in the arms trade. When she refused he made her work overtime. She kept panting by my window with her basket full of clods. Finally I went out to help and she gave me her holy scapular. Since then she's wanted me. She sends me drawings of Saint Francis with my Employee Yearbook picture taped over his face. She's sweet but too apocalyptic. You try kissing someone good-night who's just told you for the umpteenth time that the world's experiencing its last disgusting paroxysm before Rapture.

Connie comes in and I tell her I'm a Table Boy. She says it serves me right. She takes off her blouse and says that in spite of being bombarded with rocks, Corbett's decided to stay, and desires Bookish Queen Mother instead of the scheduled Ferryman's Mentally Feeble Daughter. She asks if by way of apology I'll help her suit up. I tell her no way. She puts on a push-up bra and a fake ermine robe and some horn-rims. She says Corbett's better than most, in that he's nonabusive and buys her gifts off the record. She says she thinks he's fallen for her. I accuse her of self-delusion. I ask her to reconsider for my sake and not have sex with him.

She takes my face between her hands.

"I am never, ever starving or being made a fool of again," she says. "No matter what. I'll sleep with the entire universe before I ever pick up another horse turd in a bucket."

Then she goes out the door and the Ramirez twins cross themselves in tandem and take out their checkerboard.

THE GLEASONS ARE regulars. They've got a tidy nest egg that allows them to patronize us three times a year. Mr. Gleason's an undertaker. When the first wave of mass death swept over the Northeast he got rich by inventing the Mobile Embalmer. Anyone with even a cursory knowledge of chemistry could preserve a loved one on the spot, and for a fraction of the cost associated with traditional methods.

I go in wearing my Table Boy duds and he's stretched out on a couch being fed grapes by Lydia Bell, a closet radical feminist born without eyelids who's always telling me about her secret plan to eventually slaughter some male Clients. For now she's saving like crazy and biding her time. She gets revenge in small ways, like leaving bits of stem on Gleason's grapes. Every time she does it she gives me a look. Gleason doesn't notice because he's too busy miming licking her navel whenever she reaches for her eyedrops.

After the Feast we all hustle down to the walk-in as usual to wolf down the leftovers. Before long Gleason comes wandering in drunk with a gravy splotch on his tunic and gives a speech about how fair free enterprise is. He asks what percentage of us are Flawed. I say all. He says the fact that we're not at each other's throats fighting for our daily bread but instead are squatting in a walk-in enjoying food he's paid for is testimony to the workability of this beautiful system. He leers and asks Lydia if she'd like to do some grape-feeding in a less formal setting.

Then the Perimeter Violation Alarm sounds. Lydia rushes out ahead of me, gnawing on a roaster and shading her lidless eyes. Per specs we dash to the front gate, where a dozen members of Austerity are singing minor-key hymns and throwing buckets of black paint at our retaining wall. As usual one of them is dressed as Death Eating Chips to protest the reemergence of wasteful packaging practices. Austerity considers us decadent. They hate the fact that we market opulence. They kill a cow per family per year and use every single part. They make candles from the bone marrow and pudding from the brains. They boil the fat to make soap and use the leftovers to grease their looms. Their faces are pale and they have bony knuckles from so often going around with their fists clenched. The women all look depressed and wear bonnets. In their camps everybody works. The children work and the elderly work and the handicapped work. At one camp they had a baldheaded lunatic who paced and paced while reciting Browning, so they tethered him to the water well and he wore a circular trough into the ground, but not before producing hundreds of useful gallons.

They're screaming up at us to reduce our Clients' per capita caloric intake. They're imploring us to refuse our allocated narcotics so we can see the power structure more clearly. They're calling us brothers and sisters and asking why we honor the very mind-set responsible for the world's sorry state.

Oberlin's screaming back that they're only austere because they've got no other options. Gerard, Oberlin's behemoth Security stooge, says let's turn the firehoses on the loudmouths. I fall in with the others and we wrestle the hose to the top of the wall. Gerard turns on the water and we blast Austerity back to tree line. Death Eating Chips stumbles and because of the weight of his head can't get up.

"Immerse that particular sucker in water!" Oberlin screams. "I desire you to make that costume inoperable."

So every time the guy gets up we blast him in the legs and he goes down in the mud again. The costume's coming apart. When it comes all the way apart we see that Death Eating Chips is a girl. In deference to Austerity's policy of eschewing anything even vaguely degrading to women she's shaved off her hair and plucked her eyebrows and is wearing a chest-flattening harness. Still, her beauty shines through.

We stop blasting her.

"Think!" she shouts. "Extrapolate your daily actions one-million-fold. Ask yourself if the things you do make sense. Then walk out of that Babylon and join us."

"Oh, shut up," Oberlin shouts. "Honestly."

She picks up what's left of her enormous head, then flips us off and rejoins her cowering wet friends in the grove. Singing "We Shall Overcome," they march back to their camp carrying lit homemade candles.

Gerard rolls up the hose and passes out our bonus cocaine.

"Heads out of butts, everybody," Oberlin says. "Fun's over. Unless I'm mistaken we still have valued Clients to transport back to a time of quaint enchantment."

So we toot up while jogging towards the Corkboard of Assignments, and when we get there everyone laughs at me and pelts me with their empty vials because according to the Corkboard my next Table Boy gig is a SafeOrgy.

NOBODY LIKES A SafeOrgy. A SafeOrgy fills you with longing and repulses you at the same time. We supply a sexy room modeled after a posh nineteen-fifties hotel. We offer BodyCons, since even the rich aren't above the sexually transmitted disease epidemic. They like to let it all hang out and express themselves without any worries, like in the old days. Today I walk in with my tray and seven shrink-wrapped Clients are rolling around on a heart-shaped bed with crooner music playing. We're not supposed to linger, just set the cold cuts down and get the hell out. But unfortunately a gorgeous overenthusiastic Client ruptures her seal. Our Employee Handbook requires us to perform a quick decon on the spot. There's a tank of soap mounted above the fireplace. She's all worked up however and starts groping me. I try to resist but she's strong. Nothing much really happens. She gets my earlobe in her mouth and starts sucking. That's about it. It's not unpleasant but I'm too scared to enjoy it. Finally I get her off me and manage to spray her from head to toe with soap. That cools her down. Maybe too much. As soon as she becomes aware that her boob is protruding from the shrink-wrap her cultural encoding gets the best of her and she starts looking down her nose at me.

"You reprobate Flawed animal!" she says, backpedaling and folding her arms over her chest. "This is going directly into the written summary portion of your Evaluation!"

Luckily the other members of her party are too soused to catch what she's saying so I manage to get out without being lynched. I immediately go over to Administration to explain it all to Oberlin and Albert. This could be real trouble. They could claim I molested a paying Client. They could demote me even further, to Gravedigger or Septic Tank Tech.

But to my surprise Albert tousles my hair and gives me a cube of fried meat, a true facility rarity. The last time I had meat was four years ago, when a drunken Client singled me out for my subservient attitude. Talk about a feast. Talk about being blocked up for weeks afterwards.

"Never mind about her," Albert says. "She'll live. We've got something more important to discuss with you."

"Respect," Oberlin says. "That's the quantity I hope to imbibe to you during the confab that is to follow this present preface I'm extolling. Because my feeling is strongly that a man has a right to know the whereabouts of, say, immediate family members, should their lifeplans take a strong hiatus. So congratulations! Don't therefore think of it as losing an erstwhile sister, but rather as having her gain her dream of off-site cohabitation with someone richer than any of us, is my read on this."

"What's he talking about?" I ask Albert.

"Connie," Albert says. "Corbett's bought her out of Bounty Land."

"Bought her out?" I say. "What does that mean?"

"Albert's putting this thing in a non-romantic light," Oberlin says. "Surely there's love there."

"Oh, there's love there," Albert says. "Considerable love."

"And think if you will of the ranch to which he'll take her!" Oberlin says. "A finer ranch none of us will ever see, much less have as a love nest of sorts."

"When are they leaving?" I say. "Where are they going?"

"Six hours ago," Oberlin says. "His spacious estate, you lovable boob! Taos, New Mexico! Affluent as all get-out. He's got more livestock than you can shake a stick at, and from there runs his antiseptic-swab empire! Your lucky sibling! You don't think she'll be waited on hand and foot, and eat like a true nouveau riche or captain of industry? She'll literally I feel be enmeshed in bonbons, not to mention a staff that loves her like one of their own and praises her personal attributes to the sky or what have you!"

"Are they getting married?" I say.

"Ho ho," Oberlin says. "What sweet naïveté of existing law you manifest, chum! But they're living together, and he's paying all her expenses, including the release fee due our facility, which will allow us to make considerable renovations to the Castle Six edifice, which is crumbling, so don't give me whining. This is a boon, for us and for you and for her."

"As next of kin, you'll need to sign this release," Albert says. "A mere formality."

"In her best interests," Oberlin says.

"No biggie," Albert says.

"If I don't sign," I say, "does he have to bring her back?"

"Haw," Oberlin says. "No. I fake your John Hancock, then boot your sorry heinie over the wall whence you came in over, leaving you to free-associate with the hateful rabble for an untold future time period."

"Just sign," Albert says. "It's a foregone conclusion. It's what she wanted. Here. Read this."

The letter's in Connie's hand. I can tell because all the i's are dotted with smiley faces.

"Cole honey," the letter says, "can you believe all my hard work finally paid off? He says he loves me! A rich Normal and he loves ME! He says the other men in my past don't matter, and that he wants to possess me totally forever. I'll miss you, but I know in my heart we'll meet again, hopefully at my place. A ranch! He said I could even have an economy car! Not to be haughty, but listen: Knuckle down and get something for yourself like I did. Don't be a dopey space cadet like Dad!"

She's signed it: "Love forever."

What can I do? Nothing's bringing her back. Maybe he really does love her. Maybe he's freethinker enough to see past her Flaw. Stranger things have happened. She's pretty and good-hearted and devoted and smart. Who wouldn't love her?

Oberlin rolls his eyes. Albert purses his lips.

I sign.

Goodbye Connie.

I NEVER CONSIDERED Dad a dopey space cadet. He was a simple man whose only marketable skill was selling home water-filtration units via sincerity. Finally, when the Third Panic was in full swing and every water source in the county became suspect, he started giving the units away. Mom said she considered herself as compassionate as the next person, but given our household expenses and the scarcity of the filters, a price increase seemed more in order than a giveaway. Dad said she should try to understand that other people, even ignorant people, even poor people, loved their children every bit as much as she loved hers.

"Tell me something I don't know," she said. "The point is, I don't love their kids as much as I love mine. And mine are fed with the money you make from those goddamned filters."

Dad sat on the couch, looking wistful and kooky.

"It doesn't matter now," he said, staring out at the swing set, where Sparky as usual sat in the glider, his days numbered. "The old criteria such as cash will have no meaning within a few weeks. Good works are the ticket."

"We need a gun," Mom said. "For if someone tries to take the house."

"The people who come to take the house," Dad said, "will have more guns than you can imagine."

And he was right. They had guns and riding crops and mortars. They had a sense of high moral purpose. They had the sanction of the provisional government and a portable sound system that blared "Homogeneity, Sweet Homogeneity" as they blockaded the home of any family with a Flawed member, meaning every family but the Quinces, who they blockaded for fraternizing with Flaweds, based on photographs they had of Mr. Quince teaching me to throw a knuckler. Soon the food ran out and DeAngelo ate our dog. Soon the militia wandered in without firing a shot and drove us into the night.

Mom led us on foot to Sid Pornoy's Jovial Bowling, where for months she'd been stashing food and water in a locker. Dad followed meekly, making inane guesses at the windchill.

"We're taking the Greyhound to Indiana," Mom said. "It's prosperous there. Flaweds are safe. Aunt Melanie wrote me."

"Why wasn't I consulted," Dad mumbled.

Obviously nobody was bowling. A man with a billy club was pushing a man in a silk jacket away from the snack bar.

"No kielbasa, Joel," the billy-club man said. "Not a link. No milk. Not a bun."

"You've known me my whole life," Joel said. "I'm your friend."

"Not a Pepsi," said the billy-club man. "Not a spoonful of relish. Not a sugar packet. The time has come for me to look out for me and mine."

"I am you and yours," Joel said. "We were schoolfriends. Remember the caroling parties? Remember when Oscar called Sister Nan a tub? Remember?"

"No," the billy-club man said. "I mean really me and mine. I mean Bonnie and little Kyle and me. Period. Not you. Don't touch my counter, Joel. Hit the road."

Mom loaded up the supplies and strapped the pack to Dad's back.

"Out of here," she whispered. "Out of here quickly."

In spite of the strife the stars were bright as crystal. A tailor squatted in his shopwindow with a machete and a *Newsweek*, waiting for looters. As we crossed the parking lot a van pulled up and the driver called Dad over.

"Keep walking," Mom said. "Ignore him."

"He's a fellow human being," Dad said. "Perhaps he needs our help."

The driver was a laid-off boilermaker. He talked to Dad nostalgically about what a friendly city Syracuse had been in the old days. Then he pulled a .22 and forced us into the van. He made us empty our pack. He seemed excited by our cinnamon rolls. He called Mom ma'am and let her keep her personal-hygiene effects. He took our money and he took our food.

"I'm sorry for this," he said. "I'm not a bad man. But my Leon. His little ribs are sticking way the hell out. You ever seen a starving kid?"

"Not yet," Mom said dryly.

The boilermaker's eyes teared up and the gun he was holding to Dad's head shook.

"I can't help it," he said. "I got to do it. You was smart enough to put some food aside. Anybody that smart'll be okay. Now get out. I got to go save my boy."

We got out. The van pulled away. Mom went into hysterics. She bent over double and started snorting. Whenever Dad got near her she elbowed him in the gut and said his ineptitude had killed us all.

"How dare you say that?" Dad said. "How dare you lose faith in me at a time like this?"

"Lose faith?" Mom screamed. "I've had none for months. Look at your poor children. They're as good as dead. Picture our babies in shrouds. Because of incompetence. Yours. Their father. Whom they've always looked up to."

"Stop," Dad said. "You can't take those things back once you've said them."

"Come on kids," Mom said. "I'll save you if this milquetoast won't."

And off we went.

"Goddamn it!" Dad screamed. "I've done my best!"

"Pitiful!" Mom screamed back.

Her words were lost in the wind. Hanging signs were blowing horizontal. Mom dragged us up University. Dad stood talking to himself in Sid's lot.

"Look!" Mom screamed. "Look how he lets us leave!"

She stepped into the street and put out her thumb. A couple we would get to know well picked us up. These were the Winstons, also on their way west. It was perfect. They loved kids. They were glad to be of service. They had plenty of money. Winston was a banker who'd kept his ear to the tracks and split in the nick of time with a trunkful of other people's money.

"Do you not have a father?" he asked.

"We do not," Mom replied.

Just then Dad plastered himself across the windshield.

It was the beginning of a bad ride. Dad got in and Mom folded him up in her arms and they wept together. A day later the Winstons put us out in the middle of nowhere because Mom and Dad rejected the Winstons' bright idea of a sexual foursome. I woke in the dead of night and heard Mr. Winston making the proposal.

"What I'm putting forth," he said, "is that the four of us make some memories. Become fast friends and abandon starchy old mind-sets about monogamy. The world's gone crazy. Let's do the same."

99

"The answer is no," Dad said. "And I'm surprised I'm not punching you."

"I'm afraid our hospitality is not being reciprocated, Mother," Mr. Winston said.

"Some people don't understand about reciprocity," Mrs. Winston said.

"Then out now, you people," Mr. Winston said, and hit the brakes. "End of the line."

He too had a gun. Apparently in all the world only we didn't.

So we got out.

"This is murder," Dad yelled. "It's freezing out here."

"Blah, blah, blah," said Mrs. Winston. "You had your chance. It would have been fun too, believe me."

"Really fun," said Mr. Winston. "Jeaninne's a heckcat in the bunk department."

We stood in the bitter wind and watched them pull away. As far as the eye could see was frozen marsh.

"Maybe we should have gone along with it," Mom said.

"Bite your tongue," Dad said. "There'll be other rides."

"Famous last words," said Mom.

AT MIDNIGHT I wake to creaking floorboards in the dark bunk-house. I hear the snores of my bunk bedmate, Phil Brent, an upbeat and effeminate swineherd ranked Class P, Visually Difficult to Bear, due to mottled tissue on his face and hands. He runs a workout program for other Class Ps and offers a miniseminar called Overcoming One's Woes Via Hopeful Mental Imaging. He names and compliments his pigs and cries on slaughtering day. Once as I passed the Porcine Receptacle I heard him telling two sows fighting over a corncob the story of Job. Tonight he's muttering optimistic slogans in his sleep and occasionally screaming out in abject terror.

I feel a tug on my toe and in the sudden candlelight see Doc Spanner himself, in our lowly bunkhouse for the first time ever. Spanner's the facility doctor for Flaweds. Some people are put off by his drinking. Others are put off by his shoddy personal hygiene. I'm put off by his medical track record. Once when I found him soused in a ditch he admitted to being confused by the difference between hemorrhoids and piles. Still, he did a nice job with Connie's tail infection.

"I can't live with what I know," he whispers. "Listen carefully: This Corbett's a bad egg. When he tires of a woman he sells her to slave traders. It's a pattern. There've been a number of cases. Oberlin told me. I had some deep talks with Connie at the clinic, and she struck me as a kind of a knockout and a nice girl. So I wanted you to know what she's in for."

"Can't we get her back?" I say. "Can't we just cancel the deal?"

"I expect you'd get some resistance to that from upstairs," he says. "Inasmuch as those turds have already spent the exit fee. My point is, someone working outside the system, exhibiting a little derring-do, motivated by strong emotions, might be able to effect a positive outcome. On the other hand, someone attempting to cross the Mississippi wearing a Flawed bracelet wouldn't exactly be greeted with open arms, and might indeed be greeted with open shackles."

He winces slightly at his wit, looks around, then pulls a key out of his pocket.

"My position has its little rewards," he says. "Every Flawed bracelet in this facility is within my jurisdiction. In the case of chafing and so on I'm allowed to perform a temporary Removal and apply ointment. Mr. Big Shot, eh? For this I went to med school. At any rate, this is a service I'm prepared to offer you."

I nod and hold out my wrist.

"Not so fast," he says. "First I want you to go see Lucian Bentley in Hagstrom Grove. He's recently taken sick days to visit his childhood home. He could give you an update on the state of the nation. The last thing I need is your death on my conscience. God knows I've got enough deaths on my conscience. Ha ha! So what do you say? Will you go see Lucian?"

"Yes," I say.

"Super," he says, then sighs heavily and disappears into the night.

Phil hangs his monstrous face down from above.

"I had such a dream," he says. "I dreamed that Doc Spanner came in here sober and spoke to you as an equal. Is that wild or what? Heavens."

"That's wild," I say.

AT FIRST LIGHT I take a few biscuits from my reserve and go over to Hagstrom Grove, where they send Employees who take things too much to heart and go nuts. The Grove is an untidy pen behind Administration with a dirt floor and a fifteen-foot chainlink. At mealtime they fling in sacks of black beans and let the mentally deficient slug it out. Consequently the fat loonies get fatter and the weak ones limp off to die under strips of cardboard.

I find Bentley behind a shed, wearing a filthy Hawaiian shirt and doing deep knee bends while grasping the fencing. I hold the biscuits in front of his face and he stands up.

"What do I have to do?" he says.

"Nothing," I say. "They're for you."

"Are they poisoned?" he says.

"No," I say.

"Eat one," he says.

So I do.

"Probably the others are poisoned," he says. "Eat a fraction of each."

I eat a corner off each biscuit. He looks at the remainders suspiciously, then sniffs them.

"I'm not sure it's worth it," he says. "How I wish you'd never come. Perhaps you've left the poison off of just those corners."

I begin to realize I'll doubt whatever information he gives me.

"Lick the entire biscuit," he says. "Then give them to me."

So I lick each biscuit.

"Both sides," he says.

I lick both sides of each biscuit. I give him the wet biscuits and he cracks them open and sniffs them. Then he puts them in his pocket.

"What do you want?" he says. "Now that you've failed to poison me to death."

"Information," I say. "About the outside."

He glares and grips my wrist. He licks his lips and bats his eyes and tugs on his earlobes. He keeps looking behind him. The only thing back there is Mr. Cleary, the nutso tenor, who as usual is singing the national anthem while frantically adjusting his testicles.

"I don't know you," Bentley says, "but you've given me biscuits. So I'll tell you the truth. It's beautiful and wild and not worth the risk. Strong and crazy people prevail. Some of them strapped me to a U-Haul and made use of me. If you get my meaning. And me a grandfather. My sin? None. Walking along the road. This crew had taken control of a bridge. Left me in the sun for a fortnight until some missionaries unstrapped me and applied salve. Consequently I've got no zest left. Listen: Don't budge from here. Learn to enjoy what little you have. Revel in the fact that your dignity hasn't yet

103

been stripped away. Every minute that you're not in absolute misery you should be weeping with gratitude and thanking God at the top of your lungs."

"Don't believe him," Cleary sings from behind us. "He is a liar out to confuse you. Ours is the finest nation on earth, filled with good-hearted lovers-of-life. I was out there fifteen years ago and found the rivers beautiful. At night the howling of dogs could be heard along the banks of crystalline rivers. I was young then, and in spite of my Flaw, Normal women snuck me in their back doors. Late at night they willingly showed me where on their bodies their moles were. They cooked me delicious meals and raked my back in bliss. The world was mine. The freedom made me dizzy. I'd go back in a heartbeat if I wasn't so sickly. My advice to you is: Taste the sweetness of the world. Leave this death trap, get out and live!"

Meanwhile Bentley's pulled a sheet of cardboard over his legs and is performing some additional sniffing of the biscuits. Obviously I'm going to have to decide for myself. How can you take the word of a man with biscuit crumbs under his nose and a habit of walking around holding his hand over his anus for fear of violation?

But it's really no decision. You grow up sleeping a few feet from someone, you see her little Catholic jumpers crumpled up in the corner, hear her wheezing with croup, huddle with her in the closet playing Bend the Hanger, and then you're supposed to sit idly by while she's sold into slavery?

I find Doc Spanner drinking for free at a Drawbridge Fete. I hide behind a Peasant Hut and step out as he stumbles by. He makes an odd sound in the back of his throat and lurches into a hay bale.

"Holy crap!" he says. "Scared the snot out of me. I've had a few snorts. Thank God. But good sneaking. If you set out to do what I think you're going to set out to do, you'll need to be good at sneaking. Are you? Are you going to set out to do what I think you're going to set out to do? I see by your eyes that the answer is yes! You swashbuckler! Have you ever got panache and verve and moxie! Exciting. I only wish my sister was a renegade whore about to be sold into slavery. You've talked to Bentley? Your mind's at ease?"

"Yes," I say. "I'm ready."

"Ah, youth!" he says, then removes my bracelet and hands me a prescription form with directions to Corbett's Taos estate written on the back.

"Kindly keep quiet vis-à-vis your source," he says. "If not, I may find myself Expelled and forced to care for the hateful rabble gratis in some real-world clinic. Yikes, would that ever bite! Best of luck, pal. Keep your head down. Don't write me any letters or I might get nailed."

Then he stumbles away and joins a group of Clients dropping bits of cheese down the mouthhole of a suit of armor being worn by the hapless Arnie Metz.

For the first time in twenty years I can see my entire forearm.

I go to the bunkhouse and put some bread crusts in a knapsack. I say goodbye to my bunk and shelving. Then I go out to the guardstation and climb up. What to do? Actually leave? Sacrifice my personal safety, my frame of reference, my few marginal friends, my job, my daily bread, my security, a lifetime of memories? My knees are shaking. I feel like throwing up, then hightailing it back to the bunkhouse for a nice bowl of black bean and my evening toot.

I think of Connie in shackles.

Then I jump.

And I'm free.

THE STARS JAR as I sprint down the hill. Soon I'm downwind of the tent-town stink and can hear their domestic disputes and their brats screaming in poor grammar. I'm not ten feet from their barbed wire when a few young toughs recognize my khaki as corporate issue and wrangle me down to the ground while giving me a ribbing about health care benefits and the amount of time I've spent in conference rooms.

I don't fight back. Assuming they don't kill me first, they'll catch hell from Mayor John Garibasi. Last summer when his daughter got married I took a huge risk by stealing a cake from Baked Goods and lowering it to him on an ad hoc dumbwaiter. Unfortunately Garibasi's nowhere to be seen, so for several minutes my face is down in the dirt. The toughs remove my clothes and appropriate them for their own use. They let me up and examine the cloth. I sit there gasping in my skivvies while some dispossessed women stand around gawking and critiquing my upper thighs.

"I want to talk to the mayor," I say in a shaky voice.

"You and what army?" says one of the toughs.

"Yeah," says another. "If we let everyone see the mayor who came here wanting to see the mayor, we'd have a whole lot of people seeing the mayor."

"And that wouldn't be good," says a third. "Because then the mayor would always be seeing someone. And besides, you're obviously a softie with bad motives. Or some kind of like spy guy."

Finally Garibasi shows up, wearing a threadbare blazer and carrying a surveying rod.

"Hey, hey, hey," he shouts at the toughs. "What the hell? How'd he get all bloody and naked like that?"

"We beat him up and stripped him," says one of the toughs.

"You ignorant pigs. No wonder you're not the fucking mayor," Garibasi says. "This is the guy who got Heather her wedding cake."

106

Talk about an awkward silence. Talk about a bunch of strapping lads blushing and hurriedly giving me my pants back, then retreating to their tents. Garibasi apologizes profusely. I get dressed.

"So what brings you out with us disgustos?" he says. "You taking vacation?"

"No," I say. "I quit."

"You quit that cushy gig?" he says. "You must have a screw loose. They taking applications? Ha ha! So what do you want? A little money? Food? What?"

"Whatever you can do," I say.

"Tell you the truth," he says, "I can't do much. I got to think economy of scale. I got to think: What can you do for me? Fact is, nothing anymore. You got no inside connections now. Basically you're a nobody. No offense. The cake thing, that was great. But that's past. We're not rich here. We're fucking poor. You know that. You had it good for a long time. You could look out and see us struggling. But now you're just like us. No pot to piss in. Hand-to-mouth. Wolf-at-the-door and so on. So all's I can give you at this point is a handshake and a good-luck kick in the ass. And a bed for a week or so. A bed in a leaky tent. A tent we were going to throw out anyway." Then he stops and looks at my wrist.

"Whoa up though," he says. "I don't see no bracelet, so I'm assuming you're Normal?"

"Well," I say. "Not exactly."

"Christ!" he says. "I been standing here talking to a goddamned Flawed as if he had a lick of sense. Offer withdrawn. Get your infectious ass out of here and hit the road. Now. Jesus. Disgusting."

I'm shocked. We always got along so well. In the notes he used to throw over the wall he was always saying how much he envied and admired me, and telling me long personal anecdotes about his love for his daughter. That's why I stole the cake. That's why I risked my job.

"Did you hear me, shithead?" he says. "What's your Flaw, big balls of wax in your ears? No wonder nobody respects you people. Hit the road, freak. Be thankful I'm too busy to have you rebraceleted."

I walk through the camp. Filthy babies are sitting in the mud, swatting at passing dogs. Some entrepreneur drags in a muffler and men start pounding it into sheet metal with old shoes. On the perimeter is an immaculate tent surrounded by flowers. A shrunken old woman minds a pot on a healthy little fire.

"Hello!" she says. "I can sense a hungry youngster. Come sit down and have something to eat."

"Garibasi said I shouldn't loiter," I say.

"That pup," she says. "Look at my tent and look at his town, then tell me who's got more sense, me or the mayor. I tell him: Just because we're down on our luck doesn't mean we have to live like animals. But he doesn't listen. He's too busy having dance parties and naming dirt streets after his mother."

She hands me a bowl made of cardboard and duct tape. In the bowl is stew. She says she got the vegetables in exchange for sewing and the meat in exchange for a home boil remedy. We eat at a table she earned midwifing. Afterwards she offers me a handmade toothbrush, then tells me to lie down so she can relax me with a soothing dulcimer melody.

"Pardon my boldness," she says, "but the pinkness of your wrist tells me that you're one of our Special people."

"You mean a Flawed," I say in a self-pitying tone.

"Flawed my eye," she says. "There's not a person on this earth who's not Flawed in one way or another."

Suddenly Garibasi's standing in the tent doorway.

"For example," she says. "Look at the size of this man's rear. If that's not a Flaw I don't know what is."

"Out, pal," Garibasi says to me. "You've had your meal. You've had your pep talk from Miss Know-It-All here. Now get going."

"You do have a whopping big bottom, Johnny," she says, laughing. "And you have no authority over me. Only I do."

"I got the authority," he says. "I got the fucking authority. Trash her tent."

The toughs pull up her stakes and dump what's left of her stew on the ground. Her matronly bun comes loose and her white hair falls down. They stomp on her dulcimer and shred her old photos. They splinter her hope chest and break her mosquito-repellent sticks, then stand around waiting for her to go into hysterics.

"You jokers," she says. "Do you really think you've damaged anything of value? I'll have this place looking better than any of yours again in no time. How sad. How sad that men like you exist and believe yourself strong."

"Easy for you to say," says one tough.

"Yeah, old bat," says another, and blows his nose on her comforter.

She gives him a look and he slithers away.

"I'm sorry, Sara," Garibasi says. "But you have to respect my authority."

"When you get some," she says, "I will."

She digs through the wreckage for a brush and reinstates her bun. Garibasi and his crew go off, whooping and playfully goosing one another.

"Now tell me," she says. "Where are you bound, and why?"

"New Mexico," I say. "A family matter."

"Good God," she says. "You Special people must stay out of the West at all costs. Believe me, I know, from bitter experience. My husband was Special. For years before he was born, his parents had been unwittingly drawing their water from a mutagenic well. Perhaps you have a similar story. He was born with a withered leg and a hearing loss, but a sweeter man you never met. Our son got the withered-leg gene only. But it never slowed him down any. He drew cartoon characters on his Flawed bracelet, played ball, wrestled, flirted with the girls. A blessing. So self-confident. So energetic. Too much so. The day he turned eighteen he left us a note: Mother, Dad, it said, I'm off to see the world. While he was gone the Thirteenth Amendment was repealed and the Slave Edict went into effect. A year later his body showed up on our doorstep in a wooden box. He looked ninety. A slaver in Alton, Illinois, had drugged him and sold him to an Idaho rancher."

She stops to regain her composure. I awkwardly pat her age-humped back. She regards me fiercely.

"Now what makes you think you're any different from my Addie?" she says. "Are you smarter? Stronger? Better prepared?"

"I can hide my Flaw by always wearing shoes?" I say feebly.

"Pshaw," she says. "It's these people's business to know a Flawed. They can smell a Flawed coming. They eat Flaweds for breakfast."

"She's my sister," I say. "I have to go."

"Then get out of my sight," she says in a trembling voice. "I consider you a suicide. Goodbye, dear dead boy. Our Lord has reserved a special place in Limbo for those who put an end to themselves."

"I'll be okay," I say.

"No," she says firmly. "You won't."

110

Then she turns away and starts putting her tent back together, singing "Simple Gifts" at the top of her ancient lungs.

THAT NIGHT I sleep a troubled sleep beside a fetid stream. I dream of Limbo, a tiny room full of dull people eternally discussing their dental work while sipping lukewarm tea. I wake at first light and hike through miles of failing forest and around noon arrive in a village of paranoiacs standing with rifles in the doorways of flapper-era homes. It's a nice town. No signs of plunder or panic. The McDonald's has been occupied by the radical Church of Appropriate Humility. Everyone calls them Guilters. The ultimate Guilter ritual is when one of them goes into a frenzy and thrusts his or her hand into a deep fryer. A mangled hand is a badge of honor. All the elders have two, and need to be helped on and off with their coats. There was a rash a few years ago of face-thrusting, until the national Guilter Council ruled it vain and self-aggrandizing. Guilters believe in quantifying pain. Each pain unit is called a Victor, after their Founder, Norm Victor. Each Victor earned is a step towards salvation. Having a loved one die tragically earns big Victors. Sometimes for a birthday present a wife will cheat on her husband with one of his friends in such a manner that the husband walks in and catches a painful eyeful. Once at the facility we got hold of a bootleg video of a group of cuckolded Guilter husbands talking about the difficulties of living with simultaneous rage and gratitude.

Two Guilter guys are standing against a golden arch painted gray. In Guilter epistemology the arches represent the twin human frailties of arrogance and mediocrity. One of the Guilters is violently pulling off his cuticles. Every few minutes he takes out his notebook and logs in some Victors. I say hi as I pass and he nods and winces and rips off another.

111

"Which direction is the Thruway?" I say.

"I'm not worthy to tell you," he says. "I'd probably get it all wrong. I'm lowly."

"Could you take your best guess?" I say.

"I don't think so," he says, and tears off a cuticle. "What if I misled you and you wandered for hours in the wrong direction? I'd feel horrible."

"Go ahead," his partner says. "If you feel really bad about it, to the point where you can't sleep, that's three Victors an hour."

The cuticle puller stops pulling.

"Seriously," his friend says. "New regulations."

"In that case," the cuticle puller says, "I believe you're going the right way."

"On the other hand," his friend says, "if you're now experiencing any pleasure thinking of your future Victors, that could mean you have to apply anti-Victors to your running total."

"Shut your trap," the cuticle puller says. "I'm not too keen on taking spiritual advice from someone who picks up cheap Victors by refusing to pee when he needs to."

"Its valid," the friend says. "I looked it up. Anyway, there are no cheap Victors."

"Says you," says the cuticle puller. "Says you, the king of the cheap Victor. The guy who induces no pain on himself for weeks at a time, then claims Victors for worrying about being so lazy."

"Ouch, Bryce," the friend says. "That cuts to the quick."

"Ha," Bryce says to me. "Now watch him claim Victors because I hurt his feelings."

"It's valid," his friend whines. "Pain is pain."

"Here's our ride," Bryce says.

112

A kind of bandstand on wheels comes up the street, pulled by six junior Guilters on bikes.

"We're going on a retreat," Bryce says.

"Have fun," I say.

"Not likely," says Bryce.

Then they get on the bandstand and ride off around the corner.

I walk to the window of the church and take a peek. It must have been something to go into a place like that and see somebody dishing up nice warm food instead of several women sitting bare-bottomed on coarse Welcome mats, listening to a little boy playing horrible violin. Imagine ordering one of everything on the menu and not being told no. Imagine idling in the drive-through with your sweetheart while singing along with the radio. What a beautiful country this must have been once, when you could hop in a coupe and buy a bag of burgers and drive, drive, drive, stopping to swim in a river or sleep in a grove of trees without worrying about intaking mutagens or having the militia arrest you and send you to the Everglades for eternity. I can't help but feel I was born in the wrong age. People then were giants, royalty, possessed of unimaginable largesse and unprecedented power to do good. What I wouldn't give to be drinking a Dr Pepper while driving an Edsel and listening to Muzak on a Victrola. What I wouldn't give to be allowed to procreate in a home of my own and toss a ball around with my offspring before heading off for a night on the town with my well-coiffed wife.

The country opens up, all dips and rises and cool shadowed blue places. Two tan dogs flee across a dam of sticks and mud. Birds swoop over and their shadows follow like quick black checkmarks. Just after three I reach the Thruway.

Foot traffic predominates. Every so often some elite guy chugs by in a motor vehicle, windows rolled up tight, and people fall all over themselves to either genuflect before him or lay goobers on his windshield. Legions of the sick wait to die along the shoulder. Wandering undercover bureaucrats whip out clipboards and assess odd taxes, bridge taxes and sleep taxes and taxes for if they catch you eating weeds without permission. Any weed on public property is considered a government agricultural product. If you eat a weed you're required to utilize a handy pre-addressed envelope to mail in your fee. The envelopes are kept in roadside racks that people keep pulling up to burn for firewood. What used to be exit signs are covered with government propaganda banners. One shows a smiling perfect blond girl flipping a burger. Sneaking up on her is a lustful hunchback wearing a Flawed bracelet.

KEEP THE AMERICAN GENE POOL PURE! the sign says.

If You Must Fuck a Flawed, Wear a Rubber, someone's scrawled over it.

I follow a herd of thin cattle driven by armed riders who whip the little people out of the way while chanting the name of the multinational corporation that owns the cows. I watch a tyke fascinated by the cowboys. He's so fascinated he wanders under a heifer and into the herd. His mom's at a food stall trying to buy hardtack in bulk at a good price by agreeing with the vendor that far from being unattractive, facial moles impart character. The vendor has facial moles aplenty. The kid vanishes among the cow bellies. I wait for someone to notice but no one does. So I vault over the cows and grab the kid and vault back out.

The mother hugs my neck. A crowd gathers. The vendor tries to recoup his losses by shrieking insults at the cows.

114

"You'll be steaks!" he shouts. "You'll be steaks and I'll gladly eat you, if you ever try to harm a human boy again! Hear me, fatties?"

"A man of courage," the mother sobs, 'who risked his all to save my Len."

"Forget it," I say. It's embarrassing. People are gaping. A smartly dressed stout man comes over and takes my hand.

"In these times, strange times that they are," he says, "seeing someone do something that's not patently selfish and fucked-up is like a breath of fresh air, good clean fresh air, not that any one of us would know good clean fresh air if a vial of it swooped down and bit us on the ass! Haw haw!"

Pretty soon the whole crowd's laughing. He hands out shiny quarters and confidently tweaks chins. He puts a big white arm around my shoulder.

"Life has been kind to me," he says. "So very kind. Damned kind. When I was about your age, I had an idea. I thought: These hard times have taken the wind out of our collective sails. People live like pigs. Time for a dash of luxury. And do you know what I did?"

"No," I say.

"I built mud huts for minimum wage for five grueling years," he says. "Ate bread crusts and never had an alcoholic beverage or a minute of relaxation. I worked every minute of overtime I could, cautiously saving my wages. Then do you know what I did?"

"No," I say.

"Just outside Erie, Pennsylvania, I built the most ass-kicking clean-air geodesic dome you've ever seen, and spent my last dime on rich soil and some ash saplings. Are you following me? Of course not, no offense, because that was

115

my moment in the sun, the instantaneous showing-out of *my* genius, not yours. And the culmination? Do you know it, the culmination?"

"No," I say.

"GlamorDivans," he says. "A difficult period while my ashes came to maturity. Then whammo, Sector A gets buzz-sawed, my special team of overpaid but brilliant carpenters swoops in, and before long, do you know what occupied the center of my warehouse under a special spotlight?"

"No," I say.

"Six damn GlamorDivans," he says. "Were their cushions specially handsewn by an incredibly talented seamstress I found in a rinky-dink tailor shop in Milwaukee? Yes. Did the ash shine under my spotlight like something from an earlier and more sane age? You bet. Did I tromp my ass off to identify loaded potential buyers? Yes yes yes. Did I own a car? Nope. Did I walk over five hundred miles and ultimately succeed in selling all six and buying a whole other load of ash saplings et cetera until I was the loaded and very happy man you see before you?"

"Yes," I say.

"Yes!" he says. "I thank God every day for the saga he gave me to live out. And now I say to you, because of the courage you manifested in saving that nameless little brat: Want aboard? Want to change your life forever and for better? Want to be part of the GlamorDivan Team and earn five hundred dollars a month?"

At the facility I made fifty a month and was the envy of every dispossessed who stood outside the retaining wall gaping up and swearing.

"I'll take that involuntary exhalation as an enthusiastic yes," he says.

I stand there nodding my head with my eyes watering.

116

"Here's the situation," he says. "I blame love for my woes. Not my love, but a barge guider's. Over seventy GlamorDivans, bought and paid for, hang in the proverbial lurch because my pal Sid, whom I literally dragged out of the gutter, has met the woman of his dreams and suddenly loathes travel. That's neither here nor there. What's here is, some of Buffalo's wealthiest are sitting around in their parlors even as we now speak, thinking: I hope old Blay didn't screw me out of four thousand bucks. And with each passing moment my name's sinking deeper into the muck, because buddy, I've already cashed the checks. It's routine. It's a cash-flow thing. Totally aboveboard. But all the same. My not-thin ass is in a sling, not that it hasn't been there a million times before in this catch-as-catch-can line of work, but at any rate my question to you is: Do you have a hankering to see Buffalo or make me very happy or accrue some serious money real quick? If yes to any of the above, it's on the scooter with you and let's see you use some of that coolheadedness and courage to make us some loot. Ha ha! Life is good!"

His scooter's hidden under some branches. I climb on. We fly along the side roads. He's got a sweaty back and a nice touch on the curves. Scrawny subsistence farmers gawk at us and walk away shaking their heads as our dust settles on the brims of their economy hats. Finally we reach the Erie Canal, where two armed Flaweds guard his blue barge.

"Why the weapons, you might ask?" he says. "The common man is my friend. I used to be him. But I'm not him now. You wave some beautiful household furnishings in front of the common man's nose, there's no telling what he might do. And these are *my* GlamorDivans. *My* body built those ten thousand mud huts. *My* signature went on the check for the saplings. Anybody fucks with my product, I sadly have to

117

bite their head off. Or rather you do, in my stead. Shoot their heads off, rather. Whatever. Haw!"

"Sir," I say, "I've never driven a boat before."

"Who's driving?" he says. "You're pulling. I apologize. I realize this was mule work in the old days but hey, these are the new days, so we best turn up our collars and deal with what is, what is now, the existing lemons from which lemonade may be made, eh? Ah, it's exciting to see a rich man in process. You, that is. Don't think of yourself as a surrogate mule, think of yourself as an entrepreneur of the physical."

I should have known. Mules are at a premium. Thousands have died of a bone marrow disease. The ones that lived lost the use of their legs. You'll walk past a field and there'll be fifteen or twenty of them lying on their sides braying. High-school kids get a kick out of pouring gas on them and lighting them up. It's a craze. The animal rights people do their best to prop them back up and slap on feed-bags and post anti-vandalism signs, but no sooner are they back at headquarters than the mules are either toppling over or burning.

"There's ample grub in the hold," Blay says warmly. "It's good food. I'm a man who likes to eat. And here's two bills. The rest I pay on arrival in Buffalo. Mike and Buddy know the details. Meet Mike and Buddy."

So I meet Mike and Buddy. Their Flaws are dental. Buddy was born with no teeth and Mike has twice as many as he needs. Both smile at once. It's disconcerting. I look at the barge.

A nice barge.

Mike and Buddy take a cash advance and go into town to get ripped.

"Truly nice fellows," Blay says, "albeit none too swift in the head. Between the two of them they have maybe one-third of a brain. Watch them closely. Rarely leave them alone.

118

You're to be the thinker and planner of the operation. The nerve center. The guru. The Normal."

"I'll try," I say.

"You'll succeed," he says. "I can look at you and see a winner. Dream big, win big. Stick with me. Self-actuate. It's been a pleasure meeting you. See you on the other end. I'll be the one proffering a huge wad of cash with your name on it."

He gives me a hug. What a sweet man. He likes me. He trusts me. The way his girth makes him rasp even when he's standing still is endearing.

I sit on the deck of the barge with a semiautomatic. The water's brown. As prescribed by federal regs, all inflow pipes are clearly labeled. RAW SEWAGE, says one. VERY POSSIBLY THORIUM, says another. Dusk comes, an early moon pops up over the swaying trees, the barge slips around on its tether like a mild dog happy to be tied, and I help myself to some noodles and milk.

Noodles. Milk.

Freedom, I think: very nice.

IN THE MORNING Buddy cooks eggs. They're good eggs. He gums them. Bits fly all around. Bits get on his chair and the saltshaker. Buddy and Mike fart with impunity, making a big comical show of lifting their butt cheeks. I think about participating to win their respect but then Mike says it's time to start pulling. We each take a tether. We walk in a row. It's not easy but it beats toadying to the whining rich. At nine we take a break and apply salve to our shoulders and have some bottled water. Every now and then a kingfisher pulls something out of the muck and looks askance at it and eats it anyway. Along the shore are decaying tract houses which now serve as bunkhouses for barge pullers. At noon we stop at one for

119

lunch. In the yard is a filthy man digging up potatoes with a taped-together hoe.

"Go on in, fellas!" he says. "My wife's put out a heckuva fine spread today. Mostly it's just potatoes, but she does great things with a spud. Don't take my word for it! Go in and see for yourself, by tasting some!"

Inside are nine kids and one other guest and an astounding tableful of potato-centered dishes. She's carved potatoes into crude figures. She's baked them and fried them and disguised them with sauce. She's mashed some of them into pulp and dyed them and spread them across the surface of others. Understandably the kids are husky. Everyone pitches in. The youngest walks along wiping the face of the second youngest as the second youngest carries bucket after bucket of water to the mother, who's washing and washing potatoes, then pitching them across the kitchen to identical twins, who cut them up while jabbering in pig Latin.

"Nineteen hours a day minimum!" the frazzled dirty father yells to us as he comes in. "It takes everything you've got. It absolutely kills you. I'm thirty but I look sixty. But what can you do? If you step off the treadmill for a minute you lose everything you've worked for!"

"Honey!" the wife yells from the steamy kitchen. "Stove's off!"

He grabs a wad of paper and runs in and stokes the stove. Meanwhile the kids are filling our tumblers and dusting off our shoes and toting laundry down to the Canal and hanging the finished laundry on a line that keeps snapping and being mended by a teenage boy who's wearing a tool belt and shouting orders to everyone at once. The baby starts crying and a limping child grabs a spoon and scoops up some mashed potatoes and pours on a little sugar, then sprints across the room to stuff the mixture in the baby's mouth.

"Good work, Gretel!" the sweating mother screams from the kitchen. "Now come take this scalding hot tray away!"

The other customer is an old man with a sales case, who flinches every time something crashes to the floor. Whenever the wife rushes by in a frenzy she touches his shoulder and says she's sorry everything's so crazy and not very appetizing, and he nods and flinches as something else crashes to the floor and shards of whatever broke fly across the room and the older kids scurry to pick them up before the baby crawls over and puts them in her mouth.

We fill our plates and go out into the yard and sit in relative peace among baskets and baskets of potatoes and piles of car parts and a goat who keeps looking over at us and making a hacking sound. The husband rushes out with a raw potato in his mouth and starts rebuilding an engine.

"If you want something nice, you've got to get it for yourself," he says around the potato. "I want a generator for my family. Lights at night. A fan in the summer. And I'm getting them!"

"Honey!" the wife yells from inside. "Come get the cat off the baby. It's trying to eat her bib."

"Coming, sweetie!" the husband yells, and grins and shrugs at us. "It's always something. But I've got to give it everything I got. That's my mission. My place in life. My calling. I'm no warrior. I'm no lover. I'm a plodding dad, plain and simple. But I love it!"

He sprints towards the house and trips on a bit of fence he's been mending and falls directly into a rosebush.

"Ah well!" he says as he pulls himself out. "Nobody said it was going to be easy. And this is definitely not easy. Wow. These thorns sure hurt. But hey. You've got to get up and keep on going. You snooze, you lose. Ouch. Yikes. Concentrate, concentrate."

121

"Honey," the wife screams. "The cat's standing right on the baby's tray with his paws in her food! Please don't dawdle! Cats have germs. Unless you don't mind your daughter eating cat germs!"

"You're snapping at me, love!" he shouts as he starts towards the house again. "Please don't snap!"

"Guys, don't fight!" one little girl cries out.

"Dad, God," the boy with the tools says. "Mom does so much for all of us."

"Don't correct your father," the mother screams.

"Don't scream at him," the father shouts.

"She can!" the tool boy yells. "She can scream at me if she wants! I don't mind!"

"Ah jeez," the father says, rolling his eyes at us.

"Daddy, goodness," the little girl says. "Please don't use Jesus' name as a cuss!"

"Don't correct your father," the mother says.

"Family," the father says tensely. "We have guests."

"Not many," the wife says. "Not nearly enough of them."

"Are we going to lose the house?" the little girl says. "Oh no!"

"We've got to pull together," the father says. "I call for a silent prayer moment."

They huddle in the yard. They hold hands and bow their heads. We stop eating, except for Buddy, who redoubles his efforts since it's family-style.

"Yes," the father says tearfully once they've finished praying. "With love there's always hope. With hope there's always healing. Yes. Yes."

"Honey," the wife calls as she goes back inside. "Shall we serve these gentlemen the dessert they paid for, or let them starve and then spread the bad word about our place up and down the Canal?"

122

"Yes," the father says. "No."

"All right then," the mother says. "Why not get back to work like the rest of us? Perhaps I'm missing the halo over your head that disqualifies you from having to do your share."

"This is exactly why I'm still single," Buddy says while vigorously gumming an eighth potato and catching the drool in his palm.

THAT NIGHT ON the barge I dream of Dad. I dream the iceballs on his cuffs and the dried blood on his face from when he fell trying to get us cornmeal from the Red Cross checkpoint. I dream him knee-deep in snow and cursing the Winstons.

When I dream it, I'm Dad.

Imagine: You're walking through a frozen marsh. Your kids are delirious with hunger and keep speaking aloud to imaginary savior-figures. Sitting against a tree is a snow-frosted corpse. Wild dogs have been at it. Your son puts on the corpse's coat. It's bloody and hangs to his knees. You're too tired to tell him take it off. Your wife sits on a rock to rest. You make the kids walk in circles to stay warm. You make them slap their hands against their thighs and recite the alphabet. You're scared. You love them so much. If only you could keep them safe.

Then through the trees you see lights. Up on a hillside is a neon sign and a floodlit castle tower.

BOUNTYLAND, the sign says, WHERE MERIT IS KING—AND SO ARE YOU!

Under the words is a picture of a crown with facial features, smiling and snapping its fingers. The sounds from inside are jovial. You smell roasting meat and hear a girls' choir rehearsing Bach. You run back to fetch your wife. She says she can't go on.

"It's all right," you say. "We're saved."

You drag your tired family up the slope. Because of the snow it's slick and the kids keep sliding down. At the gate a guard with a tattoo on his neck asks for your monthly income. You say things have been rough lately. He asks for an exact figure. You say zero. He snorts and says get lost. You start to beg.

"Christ," he says, "I would never beg in front of my wife and kids. That's degrading."

You keep begging. He shuts the gate and walks away fast. You stand there a minute, then start back down the hill. The kids lag behind, staring up at the sign and hating you for being so powerless. The girl picks up a frozen clod and gnaws at it. Your wife tells her stop but she doesn't listen. You hate your wife for being so powerless.

Kill me, God, you think, get me out of this.

Then there's an explosion and you tackle your family into a ditch and lie in the muck looking at the sky above the place on the hill:

Fireworks.

The fireworks get your goat and you drag the kids back up. At the retaining wall you tell them they'll understand someday. You hug them. They're so beautiful. Then you take the boy by an arm and a leg and heave him over the wall. He lands on the other side and shouts that his arm's broken.

"Daddy, don't leave me," he screams. "Why are you doing this?"

Your wife starts up the hill in despair, then gives up and sits in the snow.

Your daughter smiles sadly and offers her wrist.

Over she goes. She weighs very little. Your darling.

"He's telling the truth," she yells from the other side. "The bone's sticking out."

124

You must be a man of great courage to then turn and sprint down the hill weeping to rejoin your wife. You must be a man with great courage and a broken heart. Because until that day my father had never done a thing to hurt us. To hurt Connie or me. He loved us. On that we've always agreed. He threw us over to save us from death. He believed in people. He believed in the people on the other side of the wall.

We often wonder if he and Mom made it, and if so where they live.

WE PULL ALL the next day through a region of discolored reeds. At dinnertime we decide to eat ashore. You can get lard cubes or bundles of spiced grass at Canalside stands. At a family operation near Lock 32 they serve raccoon on a stick, with a lemon slice. Where they get lemons in this day and age I have no idea. Lowlifes are lined up behind the stand, hoping to suck a discarded rind. Raccoon bits are laid out on a card table. The vendor guarantees low heavy-metal content in the flesh. I ask how he can be so sure and he says he used to be a toxicologist. His wife confirms this and goes on and on about the number of skylights they used to have in their den. He produces a fading photo of himself holding a cage of lab rats. Meanwhile their daughter's giving me crazy eyes while skinning raccoons. The toxicologist sees me looking. He says a beautiful woman is a joy for-ever. He says a dad can't be too choosy these days. Anybody Normal who'll treat a woman reasonably well is a catch. He says it's amazing how quickly moral standards eroded once the culture collapsed. He says: Look at your marriage rate. He says: A young fellow these days doesn't think family, he thinks pokey-pokey continually.

When he says "pokey-pokey," his daughter crinkles up her eyes at me.

"Best raccoon in New York State," the mother says. The daughter nods and takes off her filthy jacket and reclines and stretches in a provocative way, managing to continue skinning raccoons. The paws go in a cardboard box. Likewise the heads. The pelts are piled neatly on the towpath for later sale to furriers.

"So," the mother says. "That's a nice shirt you have on."

"You're traveling as part of your job?" the father says hopefully.

"Not exactly," I say. "I'm going to visit my sister."

"He's going home," the mother says. "Isn't that nice? A family boy. A family boy returning home after some kind of success. You have nice clothes. Your mother will be pleased."

"A young man out in the world, making the grade," the father says. "Such a young man was I, back in the toxicology days."

"Where will you stay tonight?" the mother says. "Probably a hotel. A very nice one?"

"They stay on their boat, dodo," the father says.

"This may sound nervy," the mother says, "but we would be pleased to have you stay with us. Why not sleep on dry land?"

"Don't push him," the father says. "Let him decide."

"I'm not pushing," the mother says. "I'm inviting."

"He's not interested," the father says. "Can you blame him? We've failed to provide her with decent clothes. What man would want her?"

"She's desirable," the mother says. "But you're right. It's all a matter of presentation. Do you see the form on him? Nice clothing does that. Highlights those good strong muscles. A healthy kid."

"Yum," the daughter says.

"Appearing wanton won't help," the mother says.

"It might," the father says.

"You'll stay?" the mother says. "One night? Please? Who wants to sleep on a smelly old boat when he can have some good home cooking and play some cards?"

"Why insult him by calling his boat smelly?" the father says.

"Oh God," the mother says. "Did I ever not mean that."

"Spend some time!" the father says. "Why rush across the country without absorbing the local flavor? Nellie will take you to see the Boyhood Home of Frank Shenarkis."

"Boy will I," Nellie says, and licks her lips. Dad nudges Mom in the ribs.

"Just so a man cares for her and respects her in the proper fashion," he says. "That's all I want for my little sweetie pie."

"Take a walk, you two," the mother says. "Why the heck not? Get better acquainted. Make hay while the sun's still shining and all."

So we go for a walk.

The Boyhood Home is a pastel ranch on a street of pastel ranches. It's hard to believe America's Last Star was raised here. Just after the collapse of the national infrastructure, Shenarkis, an overweight Normal, reigned supreme on prime time with his depiction of Snappo the comical Flawed. Three times a week the entire nation tuned in. Snappo's Flaw was that he had a Siamese twin named Tubby growing out of his waist. Shenarkis, a master ventriloquist, handcrafted Tubby from polyurethane and then made a fortune kowtowing to the least common denominator. Every week Snappo and Tubby vied in vain for the love of Carmen Entwhistle, the Normal knockout who employed them to maintain her grounds. Snappo was always either getting tangled up in her vines or knocking something irreplaceable into the pool. He was a fool who knew it. He was gentle and acquiescent and mispronounced many words. All intelligent Flaweds hated him for selling us so short. Carmen came to like him for his simplicity. At the end of each episode they hugged. Whenever they hugged, Tubby would roll his eyes suggestively at Snappo. Sometimes the hugging went on and on. Finally around the time of the Detroit purges the feds yanked the show off the air because of the Flawed/Normal sexual overtones.

We walk through the Home hand in hand. We see the actual Tubby in a display case in the master bedroom, as well as the complicated harness system used to conjoin Tubby to Snappo. We hear a tape of Shenarkis doing Tubby's voice. It's an extremely frank Boyhood Home, in that they've documented Shenarkis's addiction-related demise and suicide. In his sister's room they've got the actual suit he was wearing when he wrapped his mouth around an exhaust pipe in despair over his cancellation. Nellie trembles at the photographs of his bloated corpse at Boca Raton. I pull her close. Over the PA comes Frank's familiar voice singing his theme, "Two Heads and Hearts Falling for You, Dear." I can't concentrate. She smells too good. Her lower back is too rock-hard.

Finally they shut down the Home for the night.

"I never liked his dumb show," Nellie says as we leave. "Dad said he got what he deserved for making Flaweds look halfway intelligent. But I did like the one where he thought the trombone was a scientific instrument. That one I liked because he was such a butthole."

"I know what you mean," I say.

At this point I'd say anything. Her brown arms are hot. Our palms have a little river between them. She keeps veering into me with her muscular hip.

"Through the woods?" she says.

"Is it a shortcut?" I say.

128

"Nope," she says.

Ten steps in she pulls her blouse over her head. Her chest is sun-dappled and her pit hair is blond. It all happens too fast to follow. Her breath thunders in my ear. She mounts me and screams with her mouth on mine. I feel a pebble being driven into my rear but I don't care.

Afterwards she immediately says I'm the best she's ever had. She says our kids will be darling. She says she wants me again, only naked. She pulls off my shirt. I basically lie there like a flounder on a shore. So far letting her do what she wants has been rewarding. My shoes come off. Then my socks.

She stands up naked and starts wailing at the sight of my claws.

"Jesus Christ!" she screams. "I just boinked a Flawed, Dad!"

I pick up my clothes and run through the woods. Acorns lodge in my heels. Manly fluids sail off me. In spite of the fact that she was repulsed by the real me, I find myself thinking in wonder of her breasts and the ripples in her belly. I'd gladly marry her. Doing that every night would be a reason for living. But apart from the fact that I disgust her, I'm a fugitive. I've violated Disclosure of Flaws legislation. I long to hold her tight and say: You took my virginity and made me forget my Flaw. Let me stay. I'll tape my claws, or file them down daily. We could adopt. But what's the use? I saw the look in her eyes. For the first time in years I'm truly ashamed of my claws. How I hate them. Oh for a pliers and the resolve to pluck them out once and for all.

I sneak back to the Canal. Her folks are standing in front of the barge, along with a shouting mob of townies and a sheriff with a rifle.

"The way I see it," her father says, "we're entitled to whatever's on that barge."

129

"Oh no you don't," Buddy says, almost in tears. "This barge belongs to Mr. Blay."

"Take what you want, folks," the sheriff says. "I have no abiding love for Flaweds."

"Blay's not Flawed, sir," Mike pleads. "He's Normal as the day is long, and a nice, nice man. Fax him. Ask him. Please. I beg you."

"He hires Flaweds," the sheriff says. "He hires Flaweds who haven't been fitted with bracelets and go around raping Normals."

Rape? I think. Rape? But I don't budge. I like Blay but no way I'm getting lynched for a bargeful of GlamorDivans.

The mob strips the barge clean. Buddy and Mike weep. I feel so bad. Poor Blay. No wonder Normals don't trust us. We're always screwing them over.

There's nothing to do. I could kick myself. I had sure transport west. I had a fat paycheck coming. I've let Connie down for a meaningless romp. I start walking. Far off I hear a train whistle. Then I hear bloodhounds. I run like hell through the woods and then along the tracks. A freight pulls through going slow and I run beside it. Holy cow, I think, I'm jumping a freight. I'm in a boxcar that smells like hay. I'm flying by a dark field full of baying dogs. The air smells like water and stars shine in the black Canal as we fly across a bridge.

NEXT MORNING LAKE Ontario's out the open door. The beach is littered with seagull corpses, which people are scooping up like mad for dinner. Fishmongers on the shore shriek at consumer advocates passing out pamphlets about the hazards of eating lake fish. It's Dunkirk, then Westfield, then Erie, then Girard. I lie in front of the open door, and as in a dream, the nation unfolds before me. You can imagine a hill, but an imagined hill is not actual, no clover smell rolls off it, no ugly dog chases a boy down it into a yard where a father is scratching himself before a chessboard set up across a birdbath. You can imagine sleeping Ashtabula but no justice is done the earnest faces manning the security bonfire at the crossroads. Here a drunk shouts advice to a tree, here a fire burns in a field of alfalfa, here the train whistle echoes back from a wall on which is scrawled: *Die Earnest Pricks*. Near Cleveland I see a mob pursuing a pig past a gutted Wal-Mart. Finally the pig's exhausted and stands heaving on a berm. The mob seems unsure how to proceed. Then some go-getter shows up with a crowbar. The pig takes a whack in the head, then discovers new energy and trots off again with the mob in pursuit. Fortunately at this point the train rounds a bend.

For hours we head west, through Sandusky, Port Clinton, then Toledo, where in a public park militiamen hold back the dispossessed with firearms while emptying Hefty bags of bread crusts into a fountain for public consumption. We pass through Angola and Elkhart, through fields of torched corn, then Chicago, racked with plague, where corpses are piled high in vacant lots beside the tracks and Comiskey is now an open-air penitentiary, then across the plains, where solitary people dressed in sacks wander across the horizon, reminding me of my own cursed family. Sweet-smelling dust fills the car. The nation goes on forever. I never knew. When old people said plenty, bounty, lush harvests, I put it down to senile nostalgia. But here are miles and miles of fields and homes. Nice homes. Once it was one family per. Once the fields were thick with food. Now city men assigned residence by the government sit smoking in the yards as we pass, looking out with hate on the domain of hayseeds, and the land lies fallow.

131

On the morning of the sixth day a family gets on in a hop-smelling southern Illinois town. The bearded dad offers me sunflower seeds and briefs me on his child-rearing philosophy. Discipline and other forms of negativity are shunned. Bedtimes don't exist. Face wiping is discouraged. At night the children charge around nude and screaming until they drop in their tracks, ostensibly feeling good about themselves.

"We ran the last true farm," one of the kids screams at me.

"Until the government put us out," the wife says softly. She's pretty the way a simple white house in a field is pretty.

"Now we're on the fucking lam," says a toddler. Both parents smile fondly.

"We're knowing America viscerally," says an older girl while digging at her crotch with her thumb.

"Indeed," the dad says. "My kids are at home on the American road."

"It's good for them not to be so staid," the mom says. "Get out and breathe the air."

"Live the life that's being lived," the dad says.

"Abandon the routines that conspire to force us into complacency," says the mom halfheartedly.

"Think of the memories they're accumulating," the dad says.

"Still, it wasn't a bad farm," the mom says.

"Darn it," the dad says. "Negativity, Ellie. Nip it in the bud. Remember? Forging self-love by creating a positive environment. Remember? They took our home but they can't break our spirit?"

"Sorry," the mom says. "I forgot. I mean, it was positive, because I was saying how much I liked our farm."

"Never mind," the dad says. "I love you so much."

Still, he looks tense. He goes to the door and hanging his feet out tries to teach the kids "This Land Is Your Land." The kids are busy leaning out of the speeding boxcar and lofting spit at little houses along the tracks.

"Nice shot, Josh," the dad says. "You sure nailed that garage."

"Shut up, Dad," Josh says. "When you talk to me it screws up my concentration."

"Sorry, buddy," the dad says.

At Springfield a nutty-looking guy in a dirty flannel shirt gets on and immediately divides the boxcar in half with bales. On his cheek is a burned-in crucifix.

"Some serious privacy's going to happen here or heads will roll," he announces. "I've had it with interpersonal relationships." Then he takes out a huge knife and sets it just inside his boundary. Even the wild kids shut up. He stretches out to sleep.

Once the kids get used to him, however, they resume shrieking. One little guy in coveralls keeps reaching across the border to touch the blade. Mom and Dad seem perplexed. To restrain or not to restrain? The blade looks sharp. But why risk quashing his natural curiosity?

I stay out of it. Another fifteen minutes and we cross the Mississippi.

The knife guy wakes up.

"Touch it again, you're fucked," he says to the kid, who's about five. The kid's eyes go wide.

"Just a minute," the dad says. "That's my son whose self-worth you're bandying about. Don't you remember what a special place the world was when you were tiny?"

"Don't jack with me," the knife guy says, "or I'll be pleased to cut out and eat your whiny little heart."

"Pshaw," the dad says. "Sticks and stones, my friend. That kind of confrontational attitude does nothing but make me feel a lack of respect for you."

"Keep talking, nimrod," the knife guy says, "and I'll have me a woman for free and a bunch of brats to toss off a moving train."

"Hey now," the dad says. "Hey now. Is that any way to talk to another human being?"

"Sam," the mom says, "maybe we should just drop it. Maybe we should drop it and keep the kids on our side of the bales."

"No, Ellie, I don't think so," the dad says. "My family is not something to be treated with disrespect."

"We don't want any trouble," the mom says.

"No trouble at all," the knife guy says, then picks up the knife and goes for the dad. I make a grab for his hand and the knife flies out the door. He tackles me and rolls me over and starts biting my neck. He's strong and stinks and I can feel he wants to kill me.

Oh God, I think, now I did it, I'm dead.

"Fellows, fellows," the dad says. "Violence doesn't solve problems."

"Help him, Sam," the mom yells. "That nut's going to murder him."

"I'm not sure I can do that," the dad says. "I can't have the kids see me contradict my own moral system."

"Dad," one kid shouts, "get off your ass!"

"No," the dad says gravely. "Someday you'll understand, and respect me all the more for it."

Meanwhile the loony's biting deep into my neck and I'm starting to see stars. I panic. I thrash. Then we sail out the door and my head hits something metallic and I'm out like a light.

I WAKE UP strapped to a stretcher propped against a dilapidated wet bar. Out a slit of a window is a duck on a tether near a mildewing empty built-in pool. Across the room a balding little man sits on the edge of a foldout bed, rubbing the feet of a hag sipping broth.

"Kenny," she screams, "where are you? I said fish! You call this fish? Is this all the thanks I get, you trying to scrimp on my fish?"

"He's an ass, Ma," says the man on the edge of the bed. "You'd think with all you've done for him."

In rushes another little balding man, identical to the first.

"Give her the damn fish, Kenny," says the man on the bed. "She's our mother, for crissake. Why try and starve her?"

"I doubt she'll starve, Benny," Kenny says, flinching. "That's all you two do is eat. Eat and yell at me."

From under the bedcover the woman smacks him with a length of wood. When he drops to one knee his brother knees him in the back.

"Benny, look who's awake," the mother says. "Our meal ticket."

"Welcome back to the land of the living," Kenny says kindly from the floor. "You had quite a lump on your noggin when I found you."

"Good old Kenny," Benny says dismissively. "Out wandering the tracks like an idiot."

"We know all about you, mister," the mother says. "We've had occasion to see you shoeless, Kenny and Benny and I."

"Very ugly claws," Benny says. "I almost blew chunks first time I saw them."

"That is, until we noticed the dollar signs on them," the mother says.

"What dollar signs?" Benny says dully.

"I don't mean literal dollar signs, son," his mother says. "I mean if we take this freak to Slavetown and sell him, we'll be on easy street, and we can hire someone competent to care for us instead of Mr. Sieve-Brain here. And Mr. Sieve-Brain can go back to working at the slaughterhouse and we'll be able to afford a radio and an occasional night out, like every other family on the block. But we won't invite Mr. Sieve-Brain out with us."

"Mr. Doofus," Benny says.

"Mr. Disappointing Son," the mother says. "No way will we take him with us."

"Too embarrassing," Benny says.

Kenny kneels wet-eyed, blinking madly.

"You must be hungry," he says to me in a quavering voice.

"You'll rue the day you put some Flawed ahead of your own mother!" the mother bellows. "If your father were dead he'd roll over in his grave. When I think of all the times I let you suck my breast, I'm disgusted. What a waste of milk. Oh, this is so frustrating! Fish, Kenny, fish, damn you! Get off your knees and bring me fish! I wish I could get out of this bed and spank your butt like I used to. Benny, give him one in the ass for me."

"Okay, Ma," Benny says, and nails Kenny in the rear with his foot.

"My sweet, obedient Benny," she says. "If only I would have had two sons as good. Now it's off to find a buyer for this disquieting mutant. Chair, Kenny, chair!"

Kenny quickly pulls a wheelchair from a cramped closet and awkwardly loads her in while Benny licks her broth bowl. She pulls Kenny's hair and bites his arm and curses him for being cavalier about her torso soreness. Finally Benny wheels her out while telling her how saintly she is and what a hard life she's had.

Kenny sits disconsolately on the bed.

"Boy oh boy," he says. "Am I ever the guy they love to hate. They sure can say mean things. And they sure do want me to go back to the slaughterhouse. But no way. Because I'm too dumb to keep up on bone load-up. Don't think I don't know I'm dumb. I'm dumb all right, and no doubt about it. Filbert put me on bloodsweeping, but that was hard, using squeegees and all. After that came killfloor. On killfloor they make you help them kill, and that was sad. Heck, I like collies. I like to pet them, not wave a pork chop in their faces so Terry can cut their throats. No sir, I won't go back and they can't make me. I'll run away. No I won't. That takes money. And I don't have any money. I can't run away without money because then if I get hungry I won't have any money to buy food with. So I can't run away until I get some money. And how am I supposed to?"

Then he looks at me and his eyes brighten.

"Hey," he says, "wait a minute. You're worth a lot. I could sell you. But that wouldn't be right. You're no different from me except for your feet and all. I can't do something wrong. That would be bad. But maybe I could. I could sell you. Then I'd have money. But then you'd be a slave. And that would be bad. Because I've seen them whipping those guys before. That would be mean of me to do that to you. I wonder what I should do. I can't do something mean and selfish. But if I don't, I'll have to stay here with Ma and Benny forever, and that would be bad for me. I'd be being mean to myself. And that wouldn't be good. I should love me. I should love me at least as much as I love you. And I don't even really know you. Hmm. I wonder what I should do, anyway?"

"Untie me?" I suggest. "Let me go?"

"No," he says. "That would be bad because then there'd be no hope for me and I'd get cranky and sad. You'd get sad and cranky too if your mom and brother were as mean as mine. Maybe yours are, though. How should I know? But if they are, I'll bet they sure make you sad. And when someone's sad, they want to be happy. I sure do. I sure do want to be happy. And the thing of it is, if I don't sell you, Ma and Benny will. No lie. So you're in the same boat either way. And I'm either really happy or really sad. So there you go. So I'll sell you. Ma and Benny are walking to Slavetown, so we can take the car and beat them easy. Okay? Okay? Does that sound good?"

Before I can answer he hefts my stretcher onto his back and stumbles out of the apartment. In the driveway is a plough-horse tethered to an ancient roofless Nova. Kenny slides me into the backseat and stuffs an oily rag in my mouth.

"Sorry about the bad taste of this rag and all," he says. "But we're still in Illinois and I don't want you to blow this for me. Do you know I've never even kissed a girl? Do you know I've never spent a night away from home? Because of Ma. Because of Benny, that turd. I can't believe I finally got up the nerve to call Benny a turd. What a big day for me! I wish I could call Ma a turd. But maybe that's asking too much. After all, she did give birth to me and everything. But maybe someday I'll just call her a turd without thinking, and won't that be something! I might even call her some other bad things, but I hope not, because that would be mean of me, and there's no reason to be mean or sad, now that I'm going to be free as the breeze from those two turds, Ma and Benny!"

Lying on my back I watch the sky glide by. Soon the air smells like river and I hear chattering street merchants and the clang of pots. Kenny ties the horse to a picnic table and takes the rag out of my mouth and loads me into a moldering skiff. Birds come alive on both banks as the sun drops into the river and Kenny's paddles break the pink water.

On the far bank is a fenced-in complex of trailers.

"Slavetown," Kenny says.

"I beg you, Kenny," I say. "Don't do this."

"I don't want to hear it," he says pitifully. "Why make me feel bad just when I'm finally about to do something good for myself? Please be quiet. Because I'm a softie. I'll do something dumb like let you go. I'm a dumb softie and you could easily trick me. Anyone could. Everyone does. People always have. I've taken it and taken it. It's made me sad in the heart, and that can't be good. I'm just sure God sent you to me so I could have a happier heart and really start living!"

I frantically tell my story as he rows. I tell about Mom and Dad. I tell about Connie. He sticks bits of life-jacket stuffing in his ears and sings at the top of his lungs. When we reach the bank he calls out to the guards, who wrestle me ashore.

"I don't have his paperwork and all," Kenny says. "But he's definitely Flawed. If you don't believe me, take a look at his feet."

"Please, Kenny," I say.

"Probably it won't be so bad," he says, chucking me on the wrist rope. "These folks seems nice enough."

A few buyers slide down the bank. In keeping with Disclosure of Flaws legislation one of the guards hangs around my neck a poster of a generic naked man and marks both feet with yellow highlighter. Occasionally someone asks to see my claws, then gives a low whistle and moves on as I stare out red-faced at the river. A thick man with long orange hair and bad acne pokes me in the ribs. He makes me lift a large stone and do jumping jacks and inspects my claws with a hand lens.

"Will he have his own bed?" Kenny says. "Will he get lots of time off?"

"Absolutely," the man says. "Oh my God am I ever generous with my Employees. I prefer to call them Employees. Either that or Involuntary Labor Associates. Name's Chick Krennup. For this prospective Involuntary Labor Associate, who frankly doesn't appear particularly strong, I'm prepared to offer you ninety dollars, tops."

"I was thinking more like two hundred," Kenny timidly ventures.

"Gasp!" Krennup says. "No offense, but have you been committing substance abuse on your boat? Eighty tops."

"Well, okay," Kenny says uncertainly. "Okay. I'll take eighty."

"You mean seventy," says Krennup.

"Oh," Kenny says. "I thought you said eighty."

"You're smooth," Krennup says. "Nice try. But seventy it is."

Kenny beams, proud to have been called smooth. Krennup counts three twenties into his hand. Whistling happily, Kenny rows the skiff away.

"Gracious!" Krennup says jovially once Kenny's out of earshot. "Did I ever take that asshole to the cleaners! At any rate, welcome to Missouri. You must be stiff as a board. Want out of that contraption? How about a little exercise and some lunch?"

I nod. He unstraps me, then flattens me with one blow of the oar. I struggle to my feet and he knocks me down again. He asks what I like best about myself and hits me until I admit I like nothing. Then he asks what I want from life and keeps hitting until I admit I want nothing. He asks what I treasure and love above all else and I say Connie. He hits. I say Connie. He hits. Finally I admit I love nothing. Wonderful, he says, then hits me once just for fun. Who is this Connie slut? he asks. Nobody, I say. Wrong answer, he says, she s a worthless dirtbag and you despise her. All right, all right, I say, she's a worthless dirtbag and I despise her. Then he hits me three times quick for selling Connie out so easily. He tells me to bark like a dog. I bark like a dog. He tells me to call him

Most High and eat a handful of dirt. I do so. He fits me with a new Flawed bracelet and asks me who took off my old one. I immediately implicate Doc Spanner. He scribbles Doc's name down and pledges to get it to the proper authorities.

"Now," he says. "I should tell you that, appearances notwithstanding, I am neither an angry nor a cruel man. I do not dislike you and, if truth be told, do not for an instant buy into the idea that you and your kind are somehow inferior to me, or deserving of subjugation. Nevertheless, you will observe me to be, to say the least, the proverbial harsh taskmaster. Why? you might ask. In a word: Carlotta Bins. The most beautiful woman in Missouri, who because of my rough-hewn appearance has declared herself out of my reach, unless I impress her in some less aesthetic-based arena. And I have chosen my arena, and it is to be slave trading, which will garner me money, money, money, which will translate into power, power, power, and houses, houses, houses, and a wardrobe suitable for my lady, the charmed, raven-tressed, irrepressible Carlotta. And you, sir, you are important to me, wildly important, in that the price I get for you will enter my coffers, where it will sit garnering interest until such time as it is part of an absolutely undeniable nest egg. In keeping with my stated intentions, you will spend this evening in unpleasant solitude, thereby becoming further distanced from your true self and more amenable to my every whim. This regimen of daytime beatings and lonely nights will continue until such time as there is nothing remaining of your free will and you have become the oft-cited putty in my hands, after which we will set out for Sarcoxie, where I will sell you and others of your ilk at tremendous markup."

He helps me up and guides me to a dank cage at tree line. He throws in some moldy ancient airline peanuts, then jabs me with the oar for not saying thanks. Finally he goes away. I sit ashamed in my cage. Who am I? I would have done anything to stop the hitting. Anything. So much for human dignity, I think, a few whacks in the ribs and you're calling a fat guy God and eating soil at his request. He was hitting *me,* I think: *me.* A nice guy. A friendly guy. The guy voted Least Likely to Object for three years running. Who in the world is he to be hitting me?

I long for a kind word, for a meal, for my bunk and locker, for BountyLand.

At dawn Krennup's leaning against my cage with a doughnut in his mouth. He sets his coffee down and opens the door and tells me to step out. I do so. He cracks me in the back of the legs until I'm on my knees, then tells me to get up because I'm on the clock. Then he knocks me down again and with his foot on my chest explains that per Federal Mandate 12 I'm to be compensated for my involuntary servitude. However I'm also to be charged for my food and water and for every minute he has to spend reprimanding me or beating me senseless or even thinking about me. Whatever money is left, which invariably will be exactly nothing, will be deposited in his bank account, for disbursement whenever he sees fit, which will typically be never.

He asks do I understand. Before I can answer he whacks me. After he whacks me I say I understand and it's all fine with me. He whacks me for volunteering information he didn't request, then ties me to a post near six Porta Pottis slanting like bad lime-green teeth. Every half hour he comes out and beats me up. I get no food. I get no water. Whenever I fall asleep he sends over a lackey to burn me with a match. He parades his other Flaweds by and they make fun of my claws and spit on me and tell me to quit being snotty and join the club so we can head west. I humiliate myself by telling them I'd very much like to join the club and begging

Krennup to untie me. Finally after three days he does. I'm
so happy I try to hug him and he knocks me down in the
dirt with his oar and says my cheekiness has just earned me
two additional days.

And when those two days are up I don't hug or thank him,
I meekly shuffle, I flinch, I hear voices, I drool, I follow him
into the trailer and stand on a milk crate in a crap-coated
stall, where four elderly Flaweds check me for body lice, then
dress me in coarse baggies and lead me to a wagon driven by
Mollie, a hag whose Flaw is a colossal turkeyneck.

She gives me a friendly smile while smearing antibiotic on
her wattles, then hops down and adds me to a line of thirty
Flaweds chained to the back of the wagon.

And off we go.

WE PLOD THROUGH Eureka and Pacific, camp in a foundry
parking lot, get up at the crack of dawn and start south again,
past porches overgrown with lilac and piles of junk bikes
being sold piecemeal for shack frames. It's Sullivan, Rolla,
Hazelgreen, and Sleeper, where a field behind a former mall
is full of singing teens digging roots by torchlight. The days
are a blur of fences, distant hills, senior citizens selling moist
towelettes on the shoulder. The air smells of fried chicken
and coffee, there are laughing girls on porches, tumbling
puppies chasing ducks, long tables of steaming food in the
sunlight, but none of it's for us. We get eight Sterno-warmed
pork nuggets and a sip of water a day. We get Mollie chirping
about the beauty of the land while rubbing bagbalm into our
shacklesores. You'd think we'd devise an escape plan or share
childhood memories while developing bonds of camaraderie
to last a lifetime. But no. We slander one another. We bicker.
We victimize an asthmatic ex-database guru from Detroit by
stealing his nuggets whenever he has a coughing fit.

By Lebanon I'm bleeding at the claws and Krennup's composing love songs to Carlotta while slugging brandy on the back of the wagon. We double-time through Marshfield and Strafford and get pelted with eggs by frat boys in Springfield and drenched to the bone in Mt. Vernon while waiting for Krennup to come out of a tavern. When he does it's with a mob of drunks and he makes me show my feet so they can compare my claws with an almond held by the tallest drunk, and the drunks conclude that every one of my claws is indeed bigger than the almond and give Krennup a dollar each, then tromp inside cackling while I stand barefoot in the freezing rain.

Next morning he wakes us before dawn and marches us out to the Sarcoxie slavemart, a fenced-in mudpatch behind a firebombed Wendy's.

"Best foot forward, folks," he says, giving Mollie a playful tug on the wattles. "The sooner I sell you misanthropes, the sooner I get home and wow Carlotta with the profits."

All morning I stand on a stump as buyers file by. They take souvenir photos of my claws, using pens and matchbooks for scale. They note the cracked flesh and the swelling and doubt aloud my ability to handle fieldwork. They ask can I cook. I say no. They ask can I build furniture or supervise a cleaning staff or create interesting pastries. I say no no no. By dinnertime it's just me and a set of Siamese twins and a few double amputees sitting hopefully on crates.

Krennup and Mollie glare at me from across the Sterno fire.

"Are we not going to be able to get anything for you?" Krennup says. "Are you literally worthless? Those feet are so off-putting. It's frustrating."

"Maybe we could rent a power sander," Mollie says.

144

"Not to intrude, folks," says a buyer nearby wearing a wool vest, "but you're talking to this man in awfully derogatory terms. I don't even talk to my sheep so negatively. I have half a mind to buy this fellow and turn him into a shepherd."

"If you've got fifty bucks you can turn him into dog food for all I care," Krennup says.

"Oh, come now," the man says. "What does a comment like that tell us about your self-image? Talk about an inhibitory belief system. You see yourself as someone who needs to sell someone else to a dog-food factory in order to validate yourself. And yet it seems to me that you have some very fine qualities. If nothing else, the fact that you own property says some positive things about your organizational skills and your will to power. Cut yourself some slack, friend. Come down off that cross of your own making, and believe in you!"

"Whatever," Krennup says. "Do you want him or not? Fifty, firm."

"Frankly, I abhor this slavery thing," the man says to me. "But you can't fight it. So I do my part to treat my people like human beings. My name's Ned Ventor. I consider myself to be working for change from within the system."

He shakes my hand, then slips Krennup a fifty and leads me to a wagon with padded seats, where four other Flaweds are sitting unchained drinking lemonade.

"Care for some lemonade?" he says. "Bagel? I hope these seats are neither too soft nor too hard. Please fill out a name tag. Attention all! What I usually like to do is hold a brief philosophical orientation session to get us all on the same wavelength. Any objections? Is this a good time for it? Great! Then let's begin with principle number one: I trust you. I'm not going to treat you like a slave and I don't expect you to act like one, not that I think for a minute that you would. Second principle: My sheep are your sheep. I realize that without you, the shepherds, my sheep would tend to wander all over the mountainside, being eaten by wolves or the dispossessed, not that I have anything against the dispossessed, only I don't like them eating my sheep. Principle three: If we get through the year without a lost sheep, it's party time. We'll have couscous and tortilla chips and dancing and, for the main course, what else, a barbecued sheep. Principles four and five: Comfort and dignity. You'll be getting hot meals three times a day, featuring selections from every food group, plus dessert, plus a mint. You'll each be getting a cottage, which you may decorate as you like, using a decoration allowance I'll distribute upon our arrival. Buy a lounge chair, or some nice prints, maybe even a coffeemaker, whatever, have some Flawed friends over for cards, I don't care. In fact I think it's great. You come out to the meadow next morning feeling empowered, you give your sheep that little extra bit of attention, all the better for me. My take on this is: I can't set you free, but if I could, I would. That is, I can't set you literally free. My business would be ruined, wouldn't it? But spiritually free, that's another matter. So I'll be offering meditation classes and miniseminars on certain motivational principles we can all put to work in our lives, even shepherds. For that matter, even sheep. We'll be doing some innovative sheep-praising, which you might think is nutty, but after you see the impressive gains in wool yields, I think you'll do a one-eighty. They come up and lick your hands as if to say: Hey, I like who I am. It's touching. I think you'll be moved. Any questions?"

"Where exactly are we going?" asks a petulant Flawed on my right whose name tag says Leonard.

"Great question, Leonard!" Ventor says. "You said to yourself: Look, I want to know where I'm headed. I like that. Good directedness. Also good assertiveness. Perhaps

you weren't quite as sensitive to my feelings as you might
have been, given that I should have told you where we were
headed right off the bat and so therefore feel at the moment a
little remiss and inadequate for not having done so, but what
the heck, a good growth opportunity for me, and a chance for
you, Leonard, to make yourself the center of attention, which
seems to be one of your issues, not that I'm in a position to
make that judgment, at least not yet. The answer, Leonard,
is: southern Utah. Here, take a look."

He passes around snapshots of his ranch and we sit oohing
and aahing while holding our lemonades between our knees.
It's beautiful. The skies are blue, the cottages immaculate, the
mountains white.

On my soft seat I say a little prayer:

Let this be real.

WE RIDE IN style through Joplin and Miami and Vinita and Big
Cabin. Ventor passes out sunscreen and shoots an antelope
from the wagon and gives us each a big chunk and a side-
salad with croutons. He laughs at our jokes and praises any
initiative we take and tells us about the summer picnics on his
spread, which will feature badminton and ice cream and blue-
grass music and pretty Flawed girls from other ranches who
really know how to dance. We make Tulsa. We make Sapulpa.
We make Chandler, Warwick, Luther, and Arcadia. A thou-
sand-member dog pack has just swept through Oklahoma
City and distraught cabbies are sprinkling lye on their dead
oxen while trying to trick beggars into the yoke. West of El
Reno there's a wide river and a collapsed bridge. A chalked
sign on a plywood scrap says: *Neerest ferry 200 miles south.*

"Ouch, this isn't good," Ventor says. "Not that it's bad.
Not that I'm trying to predestine our failure via negativity or
manifest an Eeyore paradigm."

We start off south along the river. Kids fishing from rotting docks turn to call us Flawed pigs. In a tent town there's a bingo game proceeding under a filthy awning.

Hidden away in a patch of reeds is a rowboat.

"Wow, talk about willing one's own reality into being," Ventor says. "Here I was just wishing we had a boat and one basically materializes! Super. I admit it's not the exact boat I was visualizing, but still it's a boat, and I for one am going to try to focus on its boatness, and not on those kind of huge gaping holes in the sides there. And while it's true we'll have to abandon our wagon and our horses and our supplies, I intend to put these losses behind me and work on viewing the fact that we now have to walk to Utah as a particularly challenging challenge I'll someday look back at while laughing sagely."

"So we're stealing this boat," Leonard says.

"No, Leonard, we're not stealing the boat," Ventor says. "We're borrowing the boat, albeit leaving it on the far bank once we've finished borrowing it."

He tells Leonard and Gene Sinclair and me to go across first and tells Leonard to row. Gene's a former schoolteacher with tremendous armpit goiters who's constantly measuring them with calipers.

"Good luck, men!" Ventor yells across the water. "Remember, I trust you implicitly!"

When we reach the far shore Gene and I pile out and Leonard starts back across.

"I have to admit this freedom would be kind of exhilarating if my goiters didn't hurt like the dickens," Gene says. "We could just walk away. Boy, wouldn't that be nervy! A guy tries to give you a nice cottage and some dignity and you bite him in the ass."

I think of Connie. I remember the autumn before the purge, when the Flaweds in our grade school were fitted with bracelets during a surprise Assembly. Connie and I stood there blinking madly as a Normal janitor named Fabrizi fired up his welding tool. At home Connie decorated her bracelet with glitter glue. Dad called her a trooper and praised her gumption, then broke down in sobs.

I get up and start jogging towards the trees.

Gene begs me to come back and swears that if it weren't for his aching goiters he'd teach me a lesson about ingratitude by beating my brains out. I cut across a granite ledge and drop into a canebrake. I hear Gene shouting to Ventor. Then there's a gunshot and some dirt kicks up at my feet and a little pine splinters to my left.

Free again, for what it's worth.

THAT NIGHT I sleep in a ditch. I dream that Mom's stroking my hair while reading me a comic book. I wake at dawn in the middle of a street market. There are jugglers and men expertly carving up big dogs and a few feet away from me a tall balding Normal selling pancakes from a cart. A couple of militia teens walk by with an entourage of eight Flaweds and a weeping Normal farmer.

"What did he do, boys?" asks the pancake guy. "If you don't mind me asking."

"Educated his Flaweds," says one of the teens. "Let them read whatever they liked. Now they're so educated they don't listen for shit and we have to keep whacking them."

"Yeah," says the other. "They want to debate every little point."

"No we don't," says a Flawed geezer, who promptly gets a gun butt in the midriff.

"So we burned down his farm," says the first teen.

"Do I ever endorse the wisdom of that decision," says the pancake guy. "You fellows are awfully youthful to be so insightful."

149

"You should have seen Todd pouring gas on the beets," says the first teen.

"I couldn't believe how hard you kicked that one kitchen chick who was shrieking while crawling away," says Todd.

"Chick was like shrieking at me," says the first teen.

"Then she bites his leg," Todd says. "I was like: Brad's hating this. He thinks this sucks."

"I was hating it," says Brad. "I did think it sucked."

"And yet you responded with remarkable restraint, by merely kicking her?" the pancake guy says. "I find that really, you know, great."

"We were going to respond by doing her in the barn," Brad says.

"But then the lieutenant comes up and goes no, because she's a virgin," Todd says. "I was like: dang."

"I was like that too," says Brad. "I was like: dang."

"We were both like: dang,' says Todd.

"So we went out and wasted all the cows," says Brad.

"Your delts looked so killer when you were slitting their udders," says Todd.

"I'll bet your delts looked killer as all get-out," says the pancake guy.

"Then asswipe here started the barn on fire when he was supposed to be flamethrowing the ducks," says Brad. "Lieutenant was pissed. Asswipe freaked."

"I didn't freak, I was bummed," says Todd. "I was bummed because the lieutenant thought I was a dick."

"You were a dick," says Brad. "You were a dick and you freaked."

"For my part," the pancake guy says, "I doubt very much that you were either an asswipe or a dick, nor do you strike me as the type of boy inclined to freak, not that I'm trying to be difficult or contradict anyone."

150

Then he tosses a pan of hot grease into the ditch and steps square on my chest and I start screaming bloody murder.

Brad puts his gun in my ear and drags me out.

"Congrats, dude," he says to the pancake guy. "You just copped a free slave."

"But I don't want a slave," says the pancake guy. "I can't afford one. I can barely keep myself in batter as it is."

"Tough bones," says Todd. "The regs require local resale by the finder. And that's you."

"God forbid I should appear neurotic or recalcitrant, boys," the pancake guy says, "but I have no idea where one sells a runaway slave."

"Try Tanner's," Todd says.

"Tanner's is a hoot," says Brad.

"Ooh la la," says Todd.

TANNER'S IS A brothel in a former Safeway. A wiry Normal in a jogging suit is counting crates of condoms in what used to be Produce.

"Don't tell me," he says. "You're in the mood for love."

"Actually I'd like to sell this Flawed," the pancake guy says, blushing.

"New flesh, Artie," the wiry guy says, and a pudge with a stun gun steps out from behind the crates. "What do you think, son? Think he'd make a good addition to Staff?"

"You know exactly what I think, Dad," says Artie. "I think that it's not very nice, forcing someone to become a prostitute against their will."

"Artie, sweet Jesus, why refer to our people as prostitutes?" the father says. "That's not a fun term. That's not a term that makes people want to let their hair down. That's a sad term. That's a term that, if anything, makes people want to put their hair back up, which means I eventually close up

151

shop and you hustle your ass home from college sans degree. Sheesh. My son the philosophical sourpuss. Looks down his nose at my line of work but sucks up the tuition like it's going out of style. Would it violate your principles too much to keep an eye on this guy for a few minutes, O Pure One? Think you could fucking manage that?"

"Fine, Dad," Artie says. "Whatever."

"We'll be in my office talking price," the father says, and steers the pancake guy into a former walk-in freezer now wood-paneled and decorated with framed posters of sweaty nude Flaweds sucking their fingers.

"Boy, I don't envy you," Artie says. "If you think Dad's mean to me, you should see how mean he is to his whores. I mean his Personal Pleasure Associates. PPAs. You should see how mad he'll get if he comes back here and finds you talking to me. He doesn't go for the idea of his whores chatting with Normals. I mean, if you want to pretend to groan in ecstasy or compliment some john's pecker, that's fine, but just talking for the sake of talking, no, he doesn't go for that. Which is exactly why I'm taking Physics at the community college. I'm getting out of the family business. Physics is hard. Really hard. But it's not at all hard compared to helping Dad beat the snot out of some PPA for accidentally calling an AR a john. Dad makes us call them ARs. Affection Recipients. Are you going to be one of the PPAs who dresses up like a girl? Or one who gets gagged and bound? Do you know yet? I guess you wouldn't. I hope you're neither. You seem like a nice guy, so I'll go out on a limb and say I hope you're just a regular old whore."

"Thanks," I say.

"This one time Mack in Security had to stun-gun this AR for getting too rough with this fragile PPA named Kurt," he says. "Mack told the AR, he said, look pal, you want to get rough, go to the Rough Room, there's no need to brutalize a tiny PPA like Kurt. But by that time the AR had a big old hole in his neck courtesy of Mack and had forgotten all about Kurt. You'd be amazed what a big old hole in your neck will do to your sex drive. My point is, did Mack ever catch it from Dad on that one! You should have seen Dad burning a corresponding hole in Mack's neck while I held poor Mack down. Did I like doing that? Of course not. But what was I supposed to do, contradict Dad in front of Mack? To tell you the truth, Dad scares me. I wouldn't be surprised if someday he didn't hold me down and burn a hole in my neck. Gosh, we probably shouldn't be going on and on like this. If Dad comes back and hears us, you'll get the pipefitters' convention for sure. So we'd better stop talking."

"Fine," I say.

"Last year at the pipefitters' convention Dad made this PPA named Earl wear a poodle suit," he says. "That was one room I did not want to go into, except I had to, because Earl had forgotten his fake bone even though it was clearly marked on the Work Order. Last thing I wanted to see was Earl in a poodle suit going woof woof woof under a big pile of naked pipefitters, but I had my instructions from Dad, the heathen. After I dropped off Earl's bone I went back to my room and studied Bernoulli's equation while sobbing quietly. People look at me and think, he's lucky, his dad's Max Tanner the rich pimp, but I tell you it's no picnic. Sometimes after writing a poem about the beauty of the stars I have to go around and change all the sheets. You think that's uplifting? You think that kind of activity nourishes your sublime nature? Well it doesn't, believe me."

Tanner and the pancake guy come out smiling.

"Artie, super news," Tanner says. "The price is right. All we need now is the physical exam."

153

"Great, Dad," Artie says weakly.

They examine my privates and make me hop in place so they can check my heart rate. They count my teeth and test my grip by making me squeeze a can filled with sand and have me read one of their brochures aloud to check for speech impediments.

"These feet worry me, Artie," Tanner says, tapping my claws with a Sharpie. "These little fuckers could be serious showstoppers. What if in the heat of passion this guy claws the crap out of some AR's leg and the AR gets gangrene and sues? Jesus. Although I suppose I could put him on drive-through hand jobs. Would you be in favor of drive-through hand jobs, Artie?"

"I'd be in favor of setting him and every other PPA in this dump free, Dad," says Artie.

"All right, smart guy, I'll do that," Tanner says. "Then you can swap your slide rule for a fucking shovel and join your peers in the sewage trench. Hah? Hah? Is that what you want, Einstein?"

"No, Dad," Artie says.

"Then let's have some thoughtful input here," Tanner says.

"He seems well suited to drive-through hand jobs," Artie says through clenched teeth.

"That's more like it," Tanner says. "Now go get him a sexy smock and some baby oil."

Then the lights go out and something blows up and suddenly Flaweds in lingerie are rushing by screaming, and swearing Normals are hopping over fallen beams with their pants around their knees. I grab Artie's stun gun and make for a hole in the wall. Outside are sycamores and clouds and tongues of flame devouring the words GIRLS GIRLS GIRLS on a fallen paper banner. A guy in a ski mask is sitting on a parking bumper trying to get a jammed gun to fire and a brothel security guard is sneaking up behind him with a billy club. So I stun the guard and drag the guy in the ski mask to a kind of clearing, where a bunch of other guys in ski masks pat me on the back and push me into a van as the Safeway collapses like a house of cards.

I'm bleeding at the knees and choking from smoke and have no idea who these people are or where I'm going, but at least I'm off the hook in terms of the hand jobs.

I LIE ALL night in the back of the van with three weeping rescued whores in nun costumes. When we finally stop we're rushed past some swaying denuded mesquites into a cave, where we're given bedrolls and wooden bowls of cold mush.

"Where are we?" one of the nuns asks.

"Texas," somebody answers, and lights a candle.

Outside the cave two Flaweds in ski masks sit on rocks near a campfire.

"Quite a mission," says one.

"Yes, Mitch, quite a mission," says the other, who's half the size of the first.

"Thanks to my leadership, we really exceeded our project goals," says Mitch.

"I don't know if I'd go that far," says the other. "We only rescued four crummy Flaweds. On top of which you left Frenchy at the scene."

"I beg your pardon?" says Mitch.

"Oh, come on," says the other. "First you got lost, then you attacked a brothel rather than a work camp, then you drove off in a panic, leaving Frenchy at the scene."

"I did no such thing," says Mitch. "Why do you insist on making up lies, Jerome? Frenchy and I had talked before the mission, and at that time he said that he might want to, you know, undertake some additional activities subsequent to the primary mission. It was a secret talk. No one else heard it. We even arranged a secret signal. As we were leaving the site, Frenchy gave me the secret signal, so I kept driving. Simple as that."

"What was the secret signal, Mitch?" Jerome says. "Begging you at the top of his lungs to please please slow down while he sprinted alongside the van weeping? You lie, Mitch. I saw the whole thing. If I hadn't been so busy putting a tourniquet on Lance I would have wrested the wheel away and saved Frenchy myself."

"Some tourniquet," says Mitch. "The cassette player in the van is ruined with Lance's blood, thanks to you."

Then they hop to their feet and put on their caps.

"Hello, Judith," says Jerome.

"Good evening, Judith," says Mitch.

"What's all this about?" says Judith, a tall woman with a sawed-off shotgun and a clipboard.

"Mitch left Frenchy at the scene, Judith," says Jerome. "The wrong scene, incidentally. We never got anywhere near the work camp."

"I've heard," says Judith. "We'll need to talk, Mitch."

"I think that's an excellent idea," Jerome says. "Somebody really needs to talk to Mitch."

"I've got something to say," Mitch says. "You people are always yapping about oppression this and oppression that, but you certainly don't seem to mind oppressing me."

"Nobody's oppressing you, Mitch," Jerome says. "Get off it. If anything, I'd say you're attempting to oppress us, by accusing us of oppressing you. Wouldn't you say so, Judith?"

"Did you hear that, Judith?" Mitch says. "Did you hear how he turned that around? It's always my fault, and if that's not oppression I don't know what is. Just because I'm one of the few rebels with an internal Flaw, you people think you can treat me like dirt. If you think a perforated duodenum is somehow less significant than an extra arm or some open facial lesions, you're just plain wrong."

"This has nothing to do with your duodenum, Mitch," says Judith. "This is strictly a performance issue."

"You want to talk performance?" shouts Mitch. "Ask this little fart where he learned to fire a machine gun! There he was, spraying friend and foe alike, this smug look on his face, and now he has the gall to accuse me of a performance issue?"

"Leave it to you to bring my size into it," says Jerome. "For your information, my size is related to my pituitary, which in turn is related to a suite of mutagenic effects, so what you've just done, whether you're man enough to admit it or not, is make fun of my Flaw, which last time I checked was exactly what we were fighting against, Mr. Shits-in-a-Bag."

"That's enough, you two," Judith says. "Mitch, go walk the perimeter."

"Who died and made her queen," mutters Mitch.

"Phil did," Judith says sharply. "And his last words to me as he died gutshot were: Continue my work."

"Oops," says Mitch. "Guess I sort of hit a nerve there."

"What else is new?" says Jerome. "Open mouth, insert foot."

"What was the first thing I did after Phil put me in charge, Mitch?" Judith demands, holding up her left arm, at the end of which is a reddened stump. "What did I do to make myself a more valuable commander?"

"Cut off your hand with a hacksaw to get your Flawed bracelet off," Mitch says, hangdog.

"That's right," says Judith. "And why did I do that, Jerome?"

"To be able to more convincingly impersonate a Normal," says Jerome, equally hangdog.

157

"Correct," says Judith. "And what was my first solo mission, post Phil?"

"You went to Denver and ingratiated yourself with a federal judge and made off with ten grand of his loot," says Mitch.

"And what did I do with the money?" says Judith. "Did I buy myself jewels? Did I flee the country?"

"No," Jerome says. "You bought weapons and food."

"That's right," Judith says. "Weapons and food. Now. If you boys have finished presenting an absolutely shameful first impression of the movement to our guests, I'll tend to my wounded."

She leaves. Mitch and Jerome flip each other off and stomp away in opposite directions.

"Nice people," says one of the nuns.

"Charming," says another.

Then an old man brings us each a cup of cocoa and a questionnaire, which we fill out by candlelight to the sound of coyotes.

IN THE MORNING the old man shakes me awake and leads me to Judith's tent. Judith's sitting outside, wearing fatigues and hair rollers and sipping coffee.

"Good morning," she says. "Welcome to freedom. I'd like to take a few minutes to tell you a little about our operation, if I may. Please have a seat."

I sit at her feet and she gives me a cup of coffee and a sugar packet and some creamer.

"Stole these on a recent raid," she says. "A little indulgence. In general, however, our resources are rather scarce. So, after a liberation, the rescued Flaweds are basically on their own. Your cavemates of last night, for example, have been sent stumbling out across the canyon in their high heels

158

with five dollars each, regrettably still wearing their habits, because we have no budget for clothing. It kills me, but it's all we can do to replenish our ammo and buy eggs from sympathetic farmers, much less subsidize jeans for liberated whores. Which brings me to you. I understand that you saved Mitch's life by stun-gunning a Normal. That was impressive. That took guts. That implies to me that you may be a fantastic potential guerrilla. What do you say? Have you ever considered joining the movement?"

In truth I didn't even know there was a movement. At BountyLand we had Maurice Rabb, a malcontent who advocated armed Flawed rebellion. Then one day he tried to burn off his Flawed bracelet and ended up with a scorched wrist and a demotion to Porcine Reproductive Services. I'd often see him in the Birthing Barn, elbow-deep in pig afterbirth, still arguing the merits of a separate Flawed state. I tell her my story. I tell her I'm not joining anything until I find out what happened to Connie.

She removes her stump and hands me a Danish with a perfectly good hand.

"Surprise, surprise," she says. "Step inside a sec."

Inside the tent are pictures of Lincoln and Che Guevara and an extra-large Baggie stuffed with spare fake stumps.

"Here's the thing," she says. "I'm Normal. Never even had a bracelet. A few years ago I looked at the movement, or what passed for a movement, and said to myself, this is no movement, this is a bunch of uninspired yahoos waiting to be led to the slaughter, except that their moribund leadership couldn't locate the slaughter if the slaughter sent up flares. So I invented a myth and invested in some fake stumps. I stopped being Lynette, a shy debutante with no marital prospects, and became Judith, the one-handed scourge of north Texas. Now every month or so I disappear and go to the bank in Lubbock and hit my trust fund and come back with a couple grand and a wild story about robbing a convenience store or seducing a senator. Is that wrong? Is a lie told in the service of good still reprehensible? These are the types of questions I ask myself every night as I apply antifungal to my hand, which is prone to infection due to these cheap stumps. But your people respect me. They work hard for me. Some have died for me. For themselves, actually, and for you, and for Connie. Ask yourself this: if you'd go through all you have to save your sister, what would you do to save a million sisters? Imagine a Connie in every town you've passed through, Connies of all ages, babies in cribs, bitter crones, pigtailed girls, children yet unborn. You could help give them dignity, a chance at careers, children, homes, husbands, peaceful dotages. Isn't that something to work towards? Wouldn't that be a way of honoring Connie's memory?"

Her memory? I think. She's not dead. At least I don't think she's dead. She may be a high-volume whore in some frontier brothel but she's not dead.

"I can see in your eyes that you're still mired down on the petty personal level," she says.

"I guess so," I say.

"Regrettable," she says, then hands me a pocket atlas and a bag of apples and tells me mum's the word on her stump and waves me out of the tent.

I START WALKING. I sneak through sleeping Amarillo and swing north through ranch country. I hear freights clanking and barbed wire humming in the wind. I see cows asleep on their feet and families of lunatics living in overturned semis. By Clayton the apples are gone and I hurry through Mt. Dora and Grenville and Capulin with a growling stomach. I eat from Dumpsters, I gnaw flowers, I find a dead deer and stuff

160

my pockets with what I can tear off. There are orange lights in ranch windows and bikes propped against willows. There are well-tended gardens and little dresses on clotheslines and once I hear a man on a ladder say *Love me?* and a woman in a tire swing answer *Always.* I wish I was Normal. I wish I lived here and could whistle my kids in from the yard as the rain made sweet homish clangings in my gutters. Instead I shiver behind a former diner and heave rocks at wild dogs and start bits of trash on fire so I can read my atlas. I limp through Raton and Cimarron and Ute Park and my mind starts to slip with hunger and the mountains speak to me in cowboy accents of the ore within them and one morning I straighten up from a gut cramp to find I'm standing in front of a sign, and the sign says: TAOS.

I eat what's left of the deer, for strength, and start down.

I get directions from some Flaweds baling hay in a meadow. I start up a dirt path. There's an orchard where they promised an orchard and a stream where they promised a stream. I crawl under some of Corbett's barbed wire, then walk through his cows and ducks and goats, practicing a little speech as I go: I know you sold her, I'll say, but I want you to know who it was that you sold. She was funny. She was thoughtful. She loved jigsaw puzzles and could do a one-arm pull-up and once saved a rabbit from a flooded culvert. She could have given you so much if you would've been man enough to accept her, but instead you deceived her and used her and turned her out for a lifetime of misery. And you'll pay. You're paying already. Because she could be here now, conferring grace on this place and on you, who could have been her savior but instead chose to be her executioner.

After that I don't know what I'll do.

The house is huge. I take a deep breath, then hop a redwood fence and land in a bed of tulips. All around my face are colored bobbing pods. There's a wet bar near a satellite dish and a trampoline near a pool.

Sitting in a rattan chair is Connie, big as a house.

Pregnant.

I look at her. She looks at me. She leaps to her feet and we do a happy little dance around the yard and Corbett steps out from behind a shrub with a croquet mallet and says that what five grand in detective fees couldn't deliver, destiny has.

Then we have lunch.

Over soup he asks if I want a job in Grounds. I say sure. Next morning he gives me a Walkman and some pruning shears. Soon I'm an old hand. I dust roses and trim shrubs and mow lawns. On my lunch breaks I read. The BountyLand library had a few Hardy Boys and a Bible with fallacious pro-slavery sayings of Christ pasted into the Sermon on the Mount, but Corbett's got everything. I read Epictetus and Frederick Douglass and Bobbo Schmidt, a Flawed Louisiana poet thrown off the Pontchartrain bridge for impregnating his Normal lover. At night Connie and I have long talks, remembering Dad's aftershave and Mom's lasagna, the swell of the hill in our yard, the names of neighbors and the voices of friends.

One night I ask her what she sees in Corbett.

"He's good to me," she says, eyes down. "I'm safe. It's not so bad."

Who am I to judge? She's here in front of me, not off suffering somewhere, not starving, not in agony, and for that I'm glad.

A week later she goes into labor in the rec room and what seems like years into the night something comes from her, something red and yowling and malleable, temporarily cross-eyed but ours, our girl, and Connie names her Anita, for our mother.

She has Corbett's eyes and Connie's vestigial tail.

That night I dream I'm standing barefoot before a crowd of hostile Normals with baseball bats. I tell them I've never loved anyone so much in my life. I describe the way the baby flinches when she passes gas, her tiny brown eyes, the smell of her head. I beg them to repeal the Slave Edict and grant her full citizenship. I ask them to consider their own children and honor that part of the eternal that resides within them. Then I stand there smiling feebly, hoping for the best, and the crowd surges forward and knocks the hell out of me with their bats until I'm dead.

I wake with a start and think: What am I doing here?

There's a rebel cell recruiting down in Talpa. According to Corbett they're a bunch of skinny passionate guys in a leaning barn, practicing hand-to-hand with broomsticks and eating vanilla wafers provided in bulk by a sympathetic grocer from Chimayó. After dinner I kiss Connie goodbye and the baby goodbye and shake Corbett's hand and off I go.

The night's cold. I see a bushel of snowfrosted apples and two black horses snorting at a frozen shirt on a fencepost and I'm lonely already.

There's a half-moon above the rebel barn. I give a little knock.

"I'm here to help," I whisper, and the door swings open.

penguin.co.uk/vintage-classics